Emmie swallowed hard and began to tremble. How could she tell him?

Isaac noticed her darkened look. "What's wrong?" he asked.

Emmie clenched her hands in her lap and silently prayed for strength. She knew she couldn't throw away everything she had ever wanted in her own strength. "I must tell you something and I don't know how," she began.

"Just say it," Isaac prompted. "I love you and nothing will change that."

"I love you, too. That's what makes this so hard." Emmie looked into his dear blue eyes and her own filled with tears at the blow she must give him. "I made a promise to Amelia, one I never expected to have to keep."

Isaac smiled in relief. "I would be glad to take her baby and love her. But I doubt that Jake would allow it."

"That's only part of it," Emmie said. "Just let me finish. Amelia thought she wouldn't survive childbirth several weeks ago. This was before you and I were engaged, before I would admit even to myself how much I loved you. She asked me to give her my word that if something happened to her I would take care of the baby and marry Jake."

The only sound for a moment was the crackling of the fire and the banging of pots in the kitchen. Isaac just stared at her as all the color drained from his face. "You promised to marry Jake?"

Emmie nodded. "And he intends to hold me to my promise."

COLLEEN COBLE and her husband, David, raised two great kids, David Jr, and Kara and they are now knee deep in paint and wallpaper chips as they restore a Victorian home. Colleen became a Christian after a bad car accident in 1980 when all her grandmother's prayers finally took root. She is very active at her church where she sings and helps her husband with a Sunday school class. She writes inspirational romance because she believes that the only happily ever after is with God at the center. She now works as a church secretary but would like to eventually pursue her writing full time.

Books by Colleen Coble

HEARTSONG PRESENTS
HP271—Where Leads the Heart

Plains
of Promise

Colleen Coble

Heartsong Presents

For my brother, Rick Rhoads,
who never let me lose faith in myself.

Thanks to my husband, David, who tirelessly followed
me around to fort after fort with good suggestions. Thanks,
honey. I couldn't have done it without you. And big hugs
to my daughter and son-in-law, Kara and Vernon Mollette,
and my son, Dave, who kept me going when the going got
tough. Thanks guys. And blessing on the head of my editor,
Rebecca Germany, who gave me a chance and so many good
suggestions. The Lord sees your hard work, Becky.

A note from the author:
I love to hear from my readers! You may correspond with me
by writing: **Colleen Coble**
                 Author Relations
                 PO Box 719
                 Uhrichsville, OH 44683

ISBN 1-57748-556-4

PLAINS OF PROMISE

Cover illustration by Lisa Peruchini.

PRINTED IN THE U.S.A.

one

The ticking of the grandfather clock in the hallway echoed in the shrouded darkness of the parlor. Emmie Courtney sat on the black horsehair sofa, her hands clasped in the folds of her silk skirt. Her violet eyes stared into space as she desperately tried to imagine she was some other place, that the reason her friends and neighbors were gathered here in her house on this sultry August day was something else entirely. The clatter of carriage wheels on the fine plank streets outside the open window thumped in time with the beat of her heart pounding in her ears.

He can't be dead. I have to wake up. This is just a nightmare. A nightmare. She repeated the litany over and over to herself as she closed her eyes to avoid the pitying eyes of her friends. Only last week her life had been perfect. Married to a handsome, up-and-coming lawyer in the rapidly burgeoning town of Wabash, Indiana, her life seemed like a fairy tale come true. The War Between the States was over, and parties and gay life were everywhere. But now her dashing husband lay newly buried in a grave under the steamy rain drizzling down outside. The nearly overpowering scent of the flowers massed around the room couldn't quite cover the stench of decay that had wafted up from the casket and permeated the room for the last few days. That undeniable smell told her quite clearly that this wasn't just a nightmare.

Her neighbor, Lally Saylors, touched her shoulder gently, and Emmie looked up. "Do try to eat a bit, Emmie, dear," Lally said with a coaxing smile. She handed her a cup of tea and a small plate with potato salad and a ham sandwich on it, then sat beside her.

Emmie took it and forced a sip of tea down her tight throat.

5

"I still can't quite grasp it, you know. I keep expecting Monroe to come bursting in the door shouting for me to get my cloak and go for a drive or something. I don't think I'll ever forget the sound of the horses screaming as the carriage rolled over."

"You were lucky to get off with only a concussion," Lally said gently.

"But Monroe—" Emmie broke off, too choked to continue.

Her eyes misting with tears, Lally patted Emmie's hand. "I know, dear."

It had been three marvelous months. Emmie had lived securely in a love that she'd never before experienced, a love that shone out of Monroe's laughing brown eyes whenever he looked at her.

"Have you thought yet about what you will do?" Lally asked.

Emmie shook her head. "I haven't heard from Ben and Labe since they left for the Dakota Territory six months ago. I don't have any other family."

"I just hate it that you're here all alone so far from your kin at a time like this."

Emmie nodded wearily. She was used to it, though. She and her brother Ben had never been close; and after her mother died when she was twelve, her father was almost always drunk until his death three years ago. She'd grown up isolated and shy in a ramshackle country home just outside town, with the animals for friends. Her brother Labe had given her sporadic attention, but Ben ignored her except when he wanted something. He had always had dreams of making the name Croftner stand for something except the town drunk. He would have approved of Monroe.

She'd never even had a best friend and didn't really know how to have fun until Monroe swept into her life like a whirlwind. They'd married after a courtship of only six weeks, and after three months of marriage, she still felt she hadn't even begun to know her fascinating husband. Now she never would.

"I'll probably stay here at least for a while," she told Lally. "The house is paid for and we never seemed to want for money. Surely there is enough to live on for a while if I'm careful. James is supposed to come out tomorrow to discuss my financial affairs." She cringed at the thought of facing Monroe's employer and his sympathy. All she wanted was to curl up here in the dark house and be left to probe her wounds alone.

Somehow she got through the funeral and the burial until all the well-meaning friends and neighbors left with promises to call again. She shut the front door wearily, then lay down on the sofa. Through the open window she heard the happy shouts of children playing hopscotch across the street and the gentle hum of the bees in the honeysuckle just under the window. The fecund scent of the Wabash River, just down the hill, wafted in with poignant memories of happy picnics with Monroe beside its placid waters. How could things seem so normal? She bit her lip as the hot tears coursed down her cheeks, then pulled the afghan down off the back of the sofa onto her shivering body. It was hot, but she couldn't stop shaking, a reaction to the trauma of seeing Monroe's casket lowered into that dark, forbidding hole in the ground.

She hadn't been able to sleep since the accident, but now she was so tired she couldn't keep her eyes open. The creaks and rattles of carriages outside on the busy street faded as she fell asleep, dreaming of Monroe's laughing brown eyes.

The parlor was deep in shadow when she awoke. She gazed around her in bewilderment, not sure what had awakened her. The clock still ticked in the hallway and carriages still rattled over the street outside. Then someone on the front porch banged the knocker again, and brushing at the wrinkles in her silk skirt, she lurched to the door. She felt disoriented and fuzzy-headed as she pulled the door open.

"Emmiline Courtney?" A young woman stood on the porch with a small boy of about two in her arms. She was neatly dressed in a dark-blue serge dress with a demure white collar.

Gentle brown eyes looked out from beneath a stylish though modest bonnet with a single, drooping ostrich feather.

"Yes. May I help you?" The child reminded her of someone, but she was still too groggy from sleep and sorrow to place who it was he looked like. And the woman's calm appraisal put her hackles up in some indefinable way.

The woman looked away from her inquiring eyes, then set her small chin and looked straight into Emmie's eyes. "May I come in? I have something of the utmost importance to discuss with you. It's about Monroe."

Puzzled over the identity of her caller, Emmie nodded and led the way into the parlor. She lit two more lamps, seated the young woman on the sofa, and sank into the matching armchair facing her guest. Discarded china from the funeral dinner still littered the smooth walnut tables.

"I'm sorry for the mess," Emmie stammered. "The funeral and all—" She broke off on a choked sob and drew a ragged breath.

Her visitor nodded as she settled the little boy on her lap and drew off her gloves.

"I'm sorry, I didn't catch your name." Emmie's gaze was caught by the pity in the woman's eyes. She caught a whiff of a faint lilac sachet as the woman pleated the folds of her dress nervously. She used to wear the scent herself, but Monroe didn't like it, so she'd switched to lily of the valley.

The young woman drew a deep breath. "This is going to come as quite a shock to you, and I'm truly sorry for that. I'm Mrs. Monroe Courtney. Catherine Courtney. Monroe was my childhood sweetheart. We were married three years ago in Cleveland."

Emmie just looked at her in puzzlement. The words had no meaning to her. How odd that they were married to someone with the same name. Then the pity in the woman's gaze penetrated her stupor. Surely the woman didn't mean she was Monroe's wife! Beginning to tremble with an awful premonition, she stared at the woman.

"Surely you wondered why he never brought you to meet his family?"

"He said they were all dead. That they died in a train accident when he was seventeen." Emmie's lips barely moved as she spoke in a whisper.

Catherine's lips tightened, and a flush stained her pale cheeks. "He has four brothers and three sisters. His mother and father are both in excellent health. They've been very hurt by his silence." She opened her reticule and drew out a picture. "Here's a family portrait of Monroe with his father and the rest of the family. It was taken just before he disappeared."

Emmie took the picture and stared down into Monroe's familiar laughing eyes. An older man with a curling handlebar mustache sat in the middle of a group of young adults. There was a marked resemblance between him and the other people in the photograph. They all had the strong jawline that made Monroe so attractive, the same large, expressive eyes.

Catherine drew a deep breath and continued with her story. "We had an argument one day. It was silly—over nothing, really. But he'd been acting restless and short tempered for several weeks. He took off, and I never heard from him again until I saw his obituary in the *Cleveland Plain Dealer*. He didn't even know about Richard here." She indicated the little boy, who had his thumb corked in his mouth. "He was never very good at responsibility. Even as a child he enjoyed pretending to be someone he wasn't. There were spells when he'd take off, but he always returned in a few weeks. This was the longest he'd ever been gone. I heard he passed himself off as a lawyer here, too. Actually he only got about halfway through law school before he grew bored and quit."

"You have proof of this?" Emmie asked, the numbness beginning to wear off. Monroe already married? Where did that leave her? She couldn't seem to take in the horror of her situation. Bigamy. The very word brought a wave of shame and nausea. Monroe had always seemed mysterious. That had been part of his magnetism. And it was true he was easily bored. But his eagerness for new adventure was part of his charm.

"I have an affidavit from his father and my marriage lines, of course. I will present them to your lawyer tomorrow."

"Then this house, his possessions, it all belongs to you," Emmie said numbly.

Catherine nodded gently. "I wouldn't have come if it wasn't for Richard. But my family is poor and Monroe's father has been supporting me and Richard. But he's struggling, too. I heard that Monroe had amassed a small holding here. It's only Richard's due that he inherit his father's possessions. You're young, and you don't have a baby to worry about. And you can always go home to your family."

Emmie wanted to burst into tears and wail aloud. But she was too numb to react. There was a certain contempt mixed in with the pity in the woman's face. Emmie was sure Catherine thought she was a fool for believing Monroe's lies.

And I was, she thought with self-contempt.

Catherine stood and pulled her gloves back on. "I'll leave you to consider all I've told you. If you need to contact me, I'll be at the Blue Goose Inn." She stared down at Emmie's face, mute with anguish and disbelief. "I'm truly sorry."

The blood thundering in her ears, Emmie watched Catherine gather her son into her arms and leave with a last, pitying look. *That's who the child looked like,* she realized with a final horror. He was a younger version of Monroe right down to the pouting upper lip. She sat rigidly in the chair with her hands clenched. What was she going to do now? There was no way to contact Ben and Labe. No one to take her in. The townspeople were kind enough, but times were too hard in the aftermath of the war for one of them to consider taking on a new burden. She couldn't ask it. This was just another instance of the feckless Croftners. She shuddered in shame. What a heyday the gossips would have with this.

Well, it was too late to do anything tonight. Tomorrow she would talk to James about her options. She blew out the lamps and climbed the open stairway to the room she'd shared with

Monroe. Repugnance overwhelmed her as she stepped into the familiar room and smelled the faint, sweet scent of Monroe's hair tonic. The big four-poster bed with its lace coverlet looked cold and alien. She couldn't sleep there, she decided. She took her nightgown and went down the hall to one of the spare rooms. The realization that she was ruined was beginning to sink in. But she couldn't think about it tonight. It would have to wait until tomorrow.

❧

Two days later, as she sat in the overstuffed chair in the law office of Taylor and Eddingfield, Emmie felt as though she couldn't handle any more shocks. Catherine had left her documents with James Eddingfield, Monroe's employer, to check. James looked through his wire-rimmed glasses and pursed his thin lips as he studied the documents.

"These seem to all be in order," he said grudgingly.

"Do I have any rights at all?" Emmie asked.

"I'm afraid not. Only what you brought into the so-called marriage. Your personal belongings and any dowry."

"I didn't have a dowry yet. When Ben's bills were settled, he told Monroe he could have what was left. The house Ben promised us as my dowry is still tied up until his debts are paid. I don't have any money until then." Ben had fled town after Rand Campbell had returned from the War Between the States and everyone discovered he had lied when he claimed Rand had died. Ben had wanted to marry Rand's fiancée, Sarah Montgomery. When the townspeople found out about his deceit, all his debts had been called in. Rather than face what he'd done, he had taken off out west.

"The law, unfortunately, is all on Catherine's side. And she does have a child to consider."

For just a moment Emmie wondered what she would do if she discovered she were pregnant also. But the thought was too shameful to consider, so she pushed it away.

James took her hand. "Is there no one who would take you in? Your brothers, perhaps?"

She didn't like the feel of his moist hand or the way he was looking at her, and she tried to discreetly pull her hand away. "No one. I don't even know where Ben and Labe are."

James squeezed her hand tighter, then lifted it to his lips. "I've always admired you, my dear Emmie. And, uh, tendered a certain regard for you. I would consider it an honor to be allowed to take care of you. There's a lovely little house on Sherman Street I own. Secluded and private. I could visit you there and see to all your needs."

The meaning of his words eluded Emmie for a few moments, but the greedy look in his eyes didn't. She gasped when she realized at last what he meant. She dragged her hand out of his grasp and rose shakily. "I thought you were Monroe's friend—and mine!"

"You're soiled goods now, my dear. What I offer is the best you can hope for once everyone knows you lived with Monroe without benefit of marriage."

"That's not my fault—I thought I was married," she whispered. She felt shamed and unclean. Was there something about her looks that made men think she was a loose woman? She'd always wondered if she was truly a Croftner. Her raven black hair and violet eyes were so very different from her brothers' fair hair and eyes.

"Perhaps. Who can say for sure what you really believed? At least that's what people will say," he said with a tight smile.

She gathered up her reticule, nausea rising in her throat, and stumbled toward the door. She had to get out of here. "I'd scrub clothes before I degraded myself like that," she whispered.

"You'll come crawling back when you see no one in polite society will accept you," he shouted as she closed the door behind her.

A half hour later, drained and disheartened, she let herself inside the cool, dark house she'd called home for three months. Mrs. Matthew must have been here while she was gone—she could smell the faint scent of lemon and wax, and the house shone as it always did after her part-time house-keeper's ministrations. It would probably be the last time Mrs. Matthew deigned to work for her once the town knew about her shame, she thought. Not that she could afford her now, of course. Her steps echoed on the oak floor as she took off her bonnet and walked wearily to the parlor. The house seemed so empty and desolate. Was it just a week ago that the house rang with voices and laughter at the elegant dinner party they'd had?

She looked around at her home. She'd brought so few personal belongings. She wouldn't even be allowed to take enough to set up housekeeping elsewhere. Just her mother's cedar chest packed with a few linens, her own clothing, and a chipped Chippendale tea set that had belonged to her grandmother.

What was she to do? Where could she go? Could she find employment here somewhere? But she had no skills, no special training. And what if James was right and she was shunned by polite society, by the very people she'd thought were her friends? She buried her face in her hands and gave into the tears she'd managed to keep at bay for the past two days. She'd tried to be strong, stronger than she felt. But fate seemed determined to keep her down in the mire. She was just the daughter of the town drunk, after all.

After a few minutes, she raised her head and wiped her cheeks. There had to be an answer to her dilemma. She bolted upright as a sudden thought took hold. What about Sarah Montgomery? She'd married Rand Campbell and followed him out west somewhere. Emmie had been so excited when Ben became engaged to Sarah, hoping that her influence would temper Ben's violent mood swings. But, of course, once Rand returned alive from the war, that engagement ended.

She'd run into Sarah's mother-in-law, Margaret, at Beitman and Wolf's dry goods counter last week. Margaret had said her daughter-in-law was pining for some female companionship; she wished she knew of some young woman to send out to keep Sarah company, she had said.

Would Sarah welcome the sister of her ex-fiancé? Sarah had always treated her like an older sister and acted as though she genuinely cared about her. She'd even sent a congratulatory letter when she'd heard of her marriage to Monroe.

Emmie rose and went to fetch her bonnet. If she hurried, she could get to Margaret's in time for lunch.

two

The stagecoach lurched and rolled its way across the arid land-scape. Emmie clutched the seat to keep from falling across the lap of the soldier sitting next to her. She still could hardly believe she was out here in the Great American Desert. The soldier had told her earlier that they should arrive at Fort Laramie today.

Catherine Courtney had given her a month to find other living arrangements. After a flurry of telegrams and last minute plans, Emmie had found herself standing in a train station about to leave for a far-off place she'd only vaguely heard of. Now, ten days later, her journey was about to end. She bit her lip and tried to still the nervous pounding of her heart.

The scenery was certainly nothing to get excited about, she thought, peering out the open window. Dry buffalo grass, sage, and weeds undulated as far as she could see in every direction. She already missed the soft greens of Indiana. No towns or settlements, just endless plains of wilderness with-out much promise.

But there was no other option except James, and almost anything was better than that. She could surely stand the isolation for a while. Then she could try to come up with another plan if this one didn't work out.

"Ever been west before, Miss?" A grizzled soldier in the seat across from her leaned forward and smiled a gap-toothed grin. His angular face was rough and reddened from the sun, and his uniform was none too clean. But he'd been friendly without being too familiar during the entire trip from Fort Leavenworth.

Emmie fanned her face and tried to keep her stomach from roiling at the stench of his breath mixed with the smell of rank, unwashed bodies and dusty leather in the tightly packed stagecoach. "Never," she said, forcing a faint smile to her pale lips.

"You ain't seen nothing until you seen them mountains out here. Lots of wide-open spaces."

The stage lurched again, and one of the soldiers up on top shouted, "Laramie up ahead!"

Emmie craned her head in a decidedly unladylike way out the window and tried to see, but the laboring horses threw up too much dust. She drew her head back in as the driver cursed at the flagging horses and urged them toward their destination. They stopped briefly at a swiftly running river, then the driver cracked the whip again and urged the team onto a waiting ferry. Her heart pounded as the fort grew nearer.

She pulled a handkerchief out of her reticule and wiped her face with it. She knew she must look terrible. Her face and neck felt gritty with cinders from the train and her scalp itched. Large patches of dust and mud clung to her skirts and shoes. She tied her blue bonnet firmly under her chin as the driver pulled the team to a halt beside a crude adobe building. Soldiers milled around outside and just across a wide parade ground Emmie could see a neat row of whitewashed adobe buildings. This was the famous fort? This nondescript assortment of rough buildings and barren wasteland? Her heart sank at the thought of living in this primitive place.

As she stepped off the stage, she gasped and almost fell when she caught sight of a throng of Indians outside the entrance to the building. She pulled her cloak tightly around her as a shield against the dangerous-looking natives. She'd heard of all the Indian atrocities just a few months ago. The papers had called 1865 "the Bloody Year."

Her garrulous soldier friend chuckled at her dismay. "They won't hurt you none. Those Injuns are Laramie Loafers. They're too dependent on gov'ment rations to cause a peep of trouble."

They looked plenty savage to Emmie. She gave them a

wide berth as she hesitantly followed the soldiers into the building. Inside even more Indians milled around. A counter made of rough wooden planks and piled with all kinds of necessities lined the back of the store, much like a general store back home. Barrels of sugar and flour and tea sat off to one side, and wide shelves behind the counter held a wide assortment of items from coffee grinders and Arbunkle coffee to ribbons and beads and boots. The smell of coffee, dust, and sweat was almost overpowering. A single kerosene lamp swung from the ceiling, and its sickly glow cast a yellowish pall over everything.

Suddenly aware that the overwhelming babble had ceased and every eye was staring at her, Emmie flushed and forced herself to approach the sutler standing behind the counter. "Excuse me, sir, but could you tell me where I might find Lieutenant Rand Campbell?"

"That lucky lieutenant always has purty wimmenfolk lookin' for him." A scrawny soldier with bright red hair stepped up beside her before the sutler could answer. "I kin take you to Sarah." He thrust out a brown hand. "I'm Lieutenant Jackson Wheeler, but you kin call me Rooster."

Emmie hesitated, then shook his hand gingerly. "I–I'm Emmie Croftner." She'd debated about what name to use and had decided on her legal one. She wanted to try to forget all about Monroe, if she could.

"Let's git out of this here crowd of buzzards. Rand and Sarah's little place is over yonder on the other side of the parade ground." Rooster opened the door for her and grabbed her satchel from her unresisting hand. "They'll be tickled pink to see you. You here to help with the wee one?"

"Yes." Emmie let the soldier ramble on. She was too tired to think or respond. She spared a quick glance around at her surroundings as she followed Rooster around the parade ground.

Soldiers stood in neat lines at attention on the parade ground as the trumpet blew a vaguely familiar tune. Two more soldiers lowered the flag from the flagpole in the middle of the field. Emmie was unable to quell the twinge of excitement and admiration at the rows of blue uniforms. There was something so masculine and attractive about a man in a uniform. Not that she was interested, of course. Between her shiftless brothers and her lying "husband," she'd had enough of men to last a lifetime. She just wanted a place to heal and a good friend to talk to.

She couldn't help gawking as she followed Rooster's spry steps. A surprising amount of activity seemed to be going on all around the fort. She could see a forest of tepees on the north side of the grounds, with squaws stooping over campfires and half-naked children shouting and running between the tepees. Horses pranced around the stable on the far side of the grounds, and beyond that, barren sage-dotted landscape stretched right up to the edge of the purple mountains in the distance.

Rooster stopped outside a neat white bungalow with a wide front porch. He bounded up the steps and pounded on the first of two doors.

Sarah opened the door with a squeal of delight and flung her arms around her. "Emmie! Oh, I'm so glad to see you. The stage must have been early—I intended to be there to meet you. Come in, come in." She drew her in and waved her thanks at Rooster before shutting the door.

Emmie hadn't seen Sarah for nearly a year. Not since she broke her engagement to Ben and followed Rand out here to this desolate place. The bright golden hair still gleamed and her green eyes still sparkled with joy and excitement. She'd gained a little weight with her pregnancy, but Emmie thought the soft roundness suited Sarah's petite femininity.

"I'm chattering like a magpie, and you must be exhausted," Sarah said. "Would you like to freshen up while I fix us a cup of tea?"

"That would be lovely. I'm just grimy from the trip." Emmie took off her bonnet and smiled at Sarah.

Sarah shuddered at the mention of the trip. "How well I remember the journey out here," she said. "Horrible food, no bathing facilities, no place to sleep. Why don't I heat some water for a bath? Rand won't be home until supper time. You can have a lovely soak."

"Sounds heavenly. But I'll get it ready if you show me where everything is. Shouldn't you be resting?"

"Now you sound like Rand." Sarah laughed. "I feel wonderful. I have a long way to go—almost four months. It will be a long wait. I'm so anxious already."

Emmie followed her through the tiny quarters. The small entry led to a parlor about ten feet square. It was a homey room with an army cot, obviously used as a sofa, that was covered with a colorful Ohio Star quilt in burgundy and blue calico and matching pillows. Warm burgundy calico curtains and matching table covers topped with lace doilies added more color. A crude table and two chairs stood under the front window and held a Bible, a copy of Shakespeare's plays, *David Copperfield,* and *Wuthering Heights.* A mantle over the fireplace held a delicate rose tea set and several small china figurines.

Just off the parlor was a small kitchen. The rough table and chairs were painted the same warm burgundy as the curtains in the parlor. Pots hung from pegs along one wall and a small cookstove sat in the middle of the room. A dry sink with a plank counter sat in one corner.

The door in the left wall of the kitchen opened into a tiny bedroom with only room for a bed and small chest. Sarah started to lift the hip bath from its peg on the wall, but Emmie quickly stepped forward and took it down herself.

"I don't want to be a bother. I'm here to help you," she scolded.

Sarah laughed as she pointed out room in the corner for the bath. "I'll heat some water."

An hour later Emmie felt like a new woman. Her dark hair shone and the lavender dress deepened the violet in her eyes.

The ladies drank their tea and ate warm bread with thick butter and jam as they chatted. The months since they last talked seemed to fall away.

Sarah sat down her teacup, and her lively smile faded. "I was sorry to hear about your husband. You were married such a short time."

Emmie carefully chewed the last bit of her jam and bread before answering. She knew she needed to tell Sarah the truth, but she didn't think she could face it yet. She'd told her she wanted to take back her maiden name since she'd been married such a short time. But Emmie was smart enough to know a secret of such magnitude never stayed hidden. There were already a few people who'd looked at her oddly in the last few days before she left Wabash.

Sarah patted her arm, her emerald eyes luminous with tears as she saw her friend's agitation. "We don't have to talk about it yet. Someday when the grief isn't so fresh and you want to tell me how wonderful Monroe was, I'll be ready to listen. It's still very difficult to talk about Papa. I still miss him so and it's been almost a year." She dabbed at her eyes with a lace-trimmed handkerchief and quickly changed the subject.

By the time Rand came home, tired and dusty, the two young women were deep in gossip from home. "I'm starving, woman," he shouted as he strode into the parlor followed by Joel, Sarah's younger brother.

Emmie didn't remember Rand very well from before the war, but she was impressed by him. He exuded a quiet strength and compassion that were unusual in a man. And he was very good looking, she thought. A shock of dark hair and expressive brown eyes, with dimples that made you want to smile with him. No wonder Sarah wasn't interested in Ben with Rand back in the picture. But how would he treat the sister of his archrival?

But her fears were groundless. Rand was the perfect host and teased her unmercifully about breaking the hearts of all the soldiers as Sarah put the delicious venison stew she'd prepared on the table. "Usually we go to officers' mess," she explained to Emmie. "But I didn't want to share you with the men your first night here. They'll be around soon enough when they hear there's a young, beautiful widow in their midst."

"They already know," Rand grinned. "I had at least ten men ask me about her. I had to tell them I hadn't seen her for over six months and she might be an ugly hag by now. I can see I was mistaken."

Emmie flushed. "I'm not interested in finding another husband," she said firmly. "Not ever." Any mention of her looks always made her uncomfortable. She knew she was very ordinary. Only Monroe had ever called her beautiful, and it was obvious now that he'd lied. Her real attraction had been the money Ben had promised.

Rand raised his eyebrows but said nothing. After supper the ladies cleared the table and washed the dishes, then followed him into the tiny parlor. He took down two harmonicas, handed one to Joel, and they began to play "Nearer My God to Thee," as Sarah sang the words in a clear, sweet soprano. Emmie knew the song a bit; it was one her father bellowed when he was drunk, so after a slight hesitation, she joined in with an alto harmony.

"That was wonderful," Sarah said, clapping her hands. "We like to have devotions together at night. We sing and Rand reads a passage of Scripture. Would you like to join us or are you too tired tonight?"

"I'd love to join you." Something about their simple, heartfelt faith pulled her. She'd always felt that God was too busy to pay any attention to someone like her. But Sarah and Rand acted like He was right there with them.

Rand picked up the worn Bible on the table by the window and flipped through the pages. "We're up to Psalms," he said, settling his broad-shouldered frame into the chair. He began to read Psalm Sixty-One in his deep voice. "Hear my cry, O God; attend unto my prayer. From the end of the earth will I cry unto thee, when my heart is overwhelmed: lead me to the rock that is higher than I. For thou hast been a shelter for me, and a strong tower from the enemy." His voice faltered and fell silent as he saw the tears sliding noiselessly down Emmie's cheeks.

"No, no, go on," she choked. "It's what I needed to hear."

As he finished the psalm, she felt a curious peace. She wanted to find out more about this personal God her friends seemed to trust so completely. This was certainly the ends of the earth like the Scripture mentioned, she thought with an inward smile.

three

Ta-dum-dum. The shrill notes of the bugle pierced the dawn air, and Emmie bolted upright in the narrow bed Rand and Sarah had fixed her in the hallway. Without sliding out of bed, she looked out the window at the top of the door. Streaks of pink heralding the day lightened the dark sky. She slid out of bed, shivering as her bare feet touched the cold floor, and padded to the door. She could hear the shouts of men across the grounds as they groomed their horses. She pushed open the door and took a deep breath of sage-scented air.

She was here at Fort Laramie, that famous bastion of might against the hordes of savages threatening the settlers trekking along the Oregon Trail. Or so the men back home said. She herself hadn't seen any threatening hordes in the short time she'd been here, just those Laramie Loafers. But there were certainly a lot of impressive-looking soldiers. She shut the door and watched through the window as the men scurried toward the mess hall. The two-story barracks across the parade ground was alive with blue-coated men hurrying toward their breakfast, then on to saddle their horses or start their fatigue duties of the day.

She poured water from the tin pitcher into the cracked bowl sitting on a cloth-covered crate. As she splashed cold water over her face and neck, she shivered. Pulling on a simple blue cotton dress, she braided her long dark hair and coiled it around her head. By the time she'd finished her ablutions, she could hear Rand and Sarah moving around the kitchen.

"Good morning," Sarah said as Emmie came toward her with a smile. "Did you sleep well?"

"I woke up a few times when somebody yelled 'All's well.' "

Sarah and Rand chuckled.

"Night watchman. You'll get used to it," Rand told her. He kissed Sarah and picked up his hat. "I'm going to be late for boots and saddles if I don't get a move on."

"Boots and saddles? What's that—some kind of war game?"

Rand grinned at the question. "That's the call to mount our horses and get on with our day. I've got to lead a detail to escort a wagon train coming in and then round up some beef for Cookie—that's what the cook's called at any fort I've ever been at. But I'll wager the men will be finding any excuse to come over here to meet you."

Rand's prediction came true. Nearly every man in the fort made some excuse to drop in over the next few days. Emmie felt strange even going outside for a walk or going to the sutler's store. Men stared at her with awe and deep respect in their eyes. It was very intimidating, especially when she felt as she did about all males. Except for Rand. He was a very nice man, God-fearing and honest to a fault. But there couldn't be two like him in the world.

Each soldier showed up hat in hand, his hair slicked back with a hair tonic that smelled of spice, blue uniform brushed and pressed. Emmie felt sorry for them, but she let Sarah deal with sending them away. Two even proposed marriage, practically in their first breath.

"I just can't stay inside another minute," Sarah announced one day after sending Joel off to school. "Can we go for a picnic?"

Rand shoveled the last bite of flapjacks into his mouth. "I guess you could. The weather has been warm, but it won't last long. You might as well enjoy it while you can. I'll see about an escort. I need to repair some telegraph line the Indians cut, but I'll send someone over. What time do you want to go?"

"About eleven. Could we go to the stream in the meadow?"

"Sure. Just don't wander off."

The girls took the laundry to Soapsuds Row, a line of tents

at the edge of the fort where a couple of enlisted men lived with their wives, who acted as the fort laundresses. The women were visiting back east right now and the men did the laundry while they were gone. After delivering their laundry, they scrubbed the tiny quarters and packed a lunch.

Promptly at eleven, someone pounded on the door and shouted in a deep baritone. "Open the door, woman. Time's a wasting!"

Emmie swung open the door and looked up into the bluest eyes she'd ever seen. The man had a friendly, open face with a shock of auburn hair that fell down over his forehead from under his blue hat. His flowing mustache matched his hair and he was quite tall, for she had to crane her neck to look up at him.

"You must be Emmie. Every man in the fort is already in love with you."

Emmie smiled in spite of her resolve to keep aloof from the soldiers. His grin was infectious. "They just haven't seen any women in a while. Who are you?"

"Isaac Liddle at your service, ma'am." He slapped the heels of his boots together and kissed her hand, then grinned again at her surprise.

She tried to place his soft accent. "I've heard a lot about you. You're Rand's best friend."

Sarah joined her at the door. "I see you've met Isaac. You behave yourself, Isaac. I don't want you scaring Emmie into leaving me."

His voice took on an injured tone. "Now, Sarah, one look at my handsome mug and she's sure to want to stay. Besides, I'm here to escort you two on your picnic. Every man in the fort clamored for the job, but I know how to get around your husband. All I had to do was promise to shine his boots for the next six months."

The girls laughed as he took the picnic basket from Sarah. "Come right this way, ladies. Your steeds await you."

The horse he selected for Emmie was a lovely buckskin

with gentle eyes. "Molly's a darling, aren't you, girl?" Isaac patted the insistent nose the mare thrust into his hand. "Have you ridden much?"

"Not really, but I like horses. We had a pony when I was little. He was an old pinto and ornery." She tentatively held out her palm and the mare gently snuffled her velvet nose against it.

"Well, Molly will be good for you. She's gentle and sweet-natured." He offered his linked hands. After a moment's hesitation, Emmie put her foot in his hands, and he helped her up onto the sidesaddle. She adjusted her skirts and gathered up the reins as he helped Sarah. Her friend's horse was a placid bay with a wide back. Rand had obviously instructed Isaac well.

Isaac led the way past the parade ground and the stables where four other soldiers joined them. As they crossed in front of the tepee village, Emmie was conscious of the black-eyed stares of the squaws and Indian children as they passed the Indian encampment. She wrinkled her nose at the pungent scent of some concoction bubbling in the pot over the open fire they skirted, mingled with dung from the numerous dogs roaming the fort area. She still hadn't been close enough to any Indians to get a good look at them. Sarah seemed to have a few friends in the group, for she waved and called to several Indian women.

The sun blazed down overhead in the brilliant blue canopy of sky. Fluffy white clouds drifted across the banner above them like lazy puffs of smoke. Emmie heard a bird cry out and looked up to see an eagle soar up into the brilliant haze above her. She felt almost as free herself. Oh, this west was a wonderful place, she thought. There didn't seem to be the strictures civilization seemed to place on you out here. It didn't feel as though someone was looking over your shoulder judging your actions constantly like back home. It was primitive, true, but she thought she was adjusting very quickly.

The meadow where they stopped was a sunny glade with a cold, clear stream running through it. The scent of sage was heavy in the air, and Isaac pointed out a prickly pear cactus for them to avoid stepping in as they dismounted and followed him to a shady spot under a cottonwood tree beside the stream.

"It's lovely," Emmie said as she spread a blanket on the mossy ground beside the stream.

"You'll love it in the spring. There are bluebells and violets everywhere." He straightened the other side of the blanket and sat down while she and Sarah opened the hamper of food. The four privates each took a separate spot in different directions and stood watch for hostile Indians. Sarah and Emmie took them a plate of food before settling down on the blanket with Isaac.

Emmie watched his face surreptitiously as they ate their lunch of cold sandwiches and baked beans. He really was a most attractive man, she decided. But she wasn't interested in getting involved with anyone. Not ever. And to be perfectly honest, he didn't seem overly smitten with her, in spite of his flirtatious manner. It was probably how he treated all women, she concluded. Teasing and indulgent like an older brother, which was fine with her.

ða

Emmie soon fell into the pattern of fort life, listening almost unconsciously for the trumpet to sound out the various calls. She didn't need the little watch pinned to her bodice anymore. Her days were divided by reveille at 5:00 A.M., breakfast at 6:00, followed by stable call at 6:30, drill at 10:00 and 2:00, retreat at 6:00 P.M., tattoo at 8:30, and taps at 8:45. She loved to watch the boots and saddles call in the morning. At the order, the cavalry swung up into their saddles in unison, the sun dancing off their brass buttons and their sabers. Then they would ride out of the fort grounds onto the open plain to practice wheeling and charging imaginary foes. It was an exhilarating sight.

After she'd been there a month and was finally beginning to settle in and feel at home, Rand came bursting in with a big grin on his face and sat in a chair beside them.

"I received new orders today."

Sarah stopped eating the dumplings made with dried apples and put her fork down. "Oh, no, Rand. Where? I don't want to go anywhere else."

His grin widened at the dread in her voice. "We're going to Fort Phil Kearny."

Sarah shrieked and jumped to throw her arms around him. He almost toppled backwards in his chair. "I get to see Amelia!" she cried as she hugged him exuberantly.

He grinned and sat the chair forward with a thump. "I thought you didn't want to go," he said with a chuckle.

Emmie watched with a pensive smile. If she could have a marriage like her friend, she might consider it, but there weren't very many men like Rand Campbell around. She pushed away the stirring of envy. What made her think she even deserved such a fine man?

Emmie knew Amelia McCallister, of course. She was the daughter of Wabash's only doctor. It was the talk of the whole town when Amelia married Jake and moved out west with him. Sarah spoke often of how much she missed her best friend, and Emmie couldn't help a stab of jealousy. Would Sarah have time for her once Amelia was around?

"When do we leave?" Emmie asked.

"You've both got two days to pack."

"Two days! You must be joking."

"They wanted me to go tomorrow, but I talked the colonel into another day in deference to you ladies. And that's quite a feat with the army. They don't even officially recognize that the wives exist usually. In the army's eyes you two are just camp followers like the ones across the river."

Emmie colored at his oblique reference to the soiled doves on the other side of the Laramie River. Rand had tried unsuccessfully to get their place of business closed down, and it was a sore spot with him. Would he put her in the same class as the prostitutes if he knew about her false marriage? She desperately hoped she'd never have to find out. Her resolve to tell Sarah the truth had faded as the days went by. She didn't want to risk seeing her friend's love and respect change to repugnance.

By working late both nights, they managed to get everything packed. Rand brought them empty pickle barrels and they packed most of their belongings in the pungent barrels, with hay packed around the breakables. Joel chattered the entire time about seeing his friend, Jimmy Carrington, again.

Both women were almost sick with excitement and nerves as they pulled out of the fort two days later. Emmie was curious to see something of the countryside. She'd already begun to chafe at the restrictions on her movements in the fort. In thirty-five days she'd only been out of the confines of the fort once on that picnic to the meadow.

They boarded the ambulance, a heavy wagon outfitted with a straw mattress and the canvas sides rolled up to let the breeze in. A canteen hung near the roof with the lid off to allow the water to cool in the breeze. Rand had rigged up a padded bench seat along each side for them to ride on, and the rest of their belongings were packed into every available inch of space. By the time they'd gone a mile, both women wished they had a horse to ride. The ambulance had no springs and they were jarred and thrown about with every pothole as they moved with the troop of nearly twenty men.

They stopped for lunch and the girls got down thankfully. Emmie drew deep breaths of sage-scented air as she bolted down the beans and bacon the cook presented. The bacon was tough so she ate around it.

"Can you bring the blanket and come with me?" Sarah whispered. "I wish there was such a thing as a portable privy."

The girls hurried off a short distance on the far side of a scraggly cottonwood tree, and Emmie held the blanket up as a screen. Above their heads the branches swayed with the breeze, and Emmie caught a whiff of some sweetly scented autumn wildflower. The gurgle of the clear creek to their right muted the sounds of the army camp behind them.

"That's one bad thing about being pregnant," Sarah said. "You can't wait very long. I don't know how I'd manage without another woman along." She hurriedly rearranged her skirts, then took her turn holding the blanket for Emmie.

"Hurry," she said. "I think they're about ready to go and I don't think they saw us leave."

By the time they started back, the ambulance was pulling away without them in it. They ran, shouting for the soldiers to stop. Rand saw them and halted the procession.

"Don't ever go off like that again without telling me," he said angrily. "We never know when we're going to run into hostiles this far from the fort. I would think you'd learned your lesson after last time, Sarah."

She flushed and tossed her head. "It didn't turn out so bad. I made some new friends."

"And almost got killed, and Jake, too."

Sarah just compressed her lips as he wheeled and rode back to the front of the line.

"What's he talking about?" Emmie was shocked at the ruckus their little necessary errand had caused.

Sarah sighed, then picked up the knitting she'd been working on before lunch. The little yellow booties she was making were half finished. "I went off by myself on a ride and Indians took me," she admitted. "But they were Laramie Loafers and it wouldn't have happened if your brother hadn't put them up to it." She stopped a moment, then sighed and went on. "They left me in a cabin for Ben, but I got away from him and some hostile Sioux found me. Little Wolverine was a young Sioux who respected Rand because of an earlier battle, and he protected me until Rand found me." She shook her head and sighed again. "Jake was injured by a bear while they were out searching for me. So now, Rand keeps a close watch on me."

Emmie could tell her friend was uncomfortable talking about Ben, but this was as good a time as any to clear the air.

The entire time since she'd arrived, she knew they both had been avoiding the subject of her brother. "So Ben did follow you. I often wondered if that's where he went." She noticed Sarah's downcast look. "I don't have any illusions about my brother's character, Sarah. I lived with him, remember?"

Sarah took a deep breath. "That's not all, Emmie. There's something I've put off telling you. I didn't want to hurt you after you'd been through so much."

"What is it?" Emmie asked after a long pause.

"I'm sorry to have to tell you that Ben was killed in a fall from his horse. Labe told Rand."

Emmie was silent. She wasn't sure how she felt about Ben, but she cared about Labe. He'd been good to her in his clumsy way. "Is Labe all right?"

Sarah nodded. "He joined up with a group of miners passing through here a couple of months ago. They were headed up the Bozeman Trail to the goldfields in Montana."

So much death. Everywhere she looked there was death, Emmie thought. First Monroe and now Ben. She wasn't sure how she came to be there, but she suddenly found herself sobbing against Sarah's shoulder. She didn't know why she was crying. She'd never been close to Ben, but he was her older brother, and now that he was gone, she was even more alone in the world. She'd probably never see Labe again, either.

By evening the wind picked up and began to moan through overhanging rocks. Black thunderheads rolled in over the tops of the bluffs and jagged flashes of lightning lit the roiling undersides.

"Get the horses tied down," Rand shouted after the supply train went into corral formation. He wheeled off on his horse, Ranger, shouting his instructions to the rest of the soldiers.

The wind struck with a fearful punch as Emmie struggled to unroll one side of the canvas covering for the ambulance while Sarah fought with the other side. Sharp needles of cold rain pelted them before they could get the bedding covered, and Emmie could barely see through her thick wet hair hanging across her face. Looming out of the driving rain, Rand dashed to secure the canvas on Sarah's side. Emmie frantically pushed her wet hair from her eyes and fought the rope holding the canvas in place. She almost shrieked as strong hands gently pushed her out of the way and fastened the canvas down with deft, practiced movements.

"Isaac," she gasped. "Where did you come from?"

He grinned, his blue eyes dancing with merriment. "I've been on ahead scouting. You didn't think I would let a pretty gal like you get away, did you?"

She flushed. Was he making fun of her? She certainly didn't feel very pretty right now with her hair plastered to her head and her dress covered with mud. And he always seemed to put her at a disadvantage.

Isaac didn't seem to notice her embarrassment. He just patted the top of her head and strode off to help the rest of the men secure everything.

Emmie pulled her shawl around her protectively. He'd patted her like—like she was a dog or a child. Was that how he saw her? She pushed away the prick of hurt and climbed back into the ambulance.

The storm cleared quickly and the procession moved on. Emmie found her eyes straying more often than she liked to Isaac's erect figure on the bay gelding. His burnished hair curled over his collar, and he was easy to pick out of the group. He seemed to have a kind and encouraging word for everyone. All the more reason for her not to believe him when he said she was beautiful. He was evidently one of those people who looked for the good in everyone. An admirable quality, she had to admit, but it made her more cautious.

"You ready to go back to Indiana?" Sarah asked when they took a short break in the middle of the afternoon.

"I thought about it," Emmie admitted. "This wilderness is a fearful place. Even the storms are wilder." Then she smiled. "But it is beautiful in a wild and savage way. I love the scent of sage in the wind and the deep, rich reds and browns of the earth. And I can't wait to get a closer look at the mountains."

They saw wildlife everywhere. Elk, deer, jackrabbit, and once a small herd of buffalo off in the distance. Emmie wanted to get a closer look at the famous beast, but they never came close enough to see well.

"That's why the Indians are so set on keeping this area," Sarah told her when she mentioned the abundant game. "And since the Montana gold mines opened up and miners keep traipsing through on the Bozeman Trail, the game is beginning to thin out. Red Cloud is said to be gathering a large war band up in the Powder River area. He's promised a fight to the knife. Rand doesn't know where it will all end. He sees the Indians' point of view, but he knows we have to expand clear to the Pacific if this nation is going to thrive. We need the railroad completed and the telegraph to all cities. The Indians won't stand by and see it happen without a fight." She shivered. "It scares me when I think about it. Every time Rand goes out on detail, I'm terrified he won't come back."

Emmie hadn't realized it was so dangerous. So far she hadn't seen a single hostile Indian. It was hard to imagine that the problem was as severe as Sarah said.

Rand called a halt around six o'clock. After beating the brush for rattlesnakes, three men pitched a tepee-like structure called a Sibley tent for the ladies.

"What are you doing?" Emmie asked Rooster as he uncoiled a large horsehair rope.

"Snakes won't cross a horsehair rope," he said, laying it on the ground all around the tent and bedrolls. "Reckon they don't like them hairs ticklin' their bellies. Rattlers ain't nothin' to mess with and we don't want to lose our only wimmenfolk. 'Course it's late in the year fer snakes, but it's so much warmer than usual, I don't 'tend to take any chances."

Emmie wasn't sure if he was telling the truth, but his words sounded comforting, so she and Sarah carried their clothes and blankets inside and tried to make the interior comfortable. When they came out of the tent, one of the men had gotten a blazing fire going. The aroma of stew made Emmie's mouth water. She had hardly touched her lunch, but now she was famished. She ate two plates of the delicious stew and washed it down with the water in the battered tin cup Rooster gave her.

While four of the men went off to stand guard duty after supper, Rand brought out the harmonicas. The plaintive notes of "Home Sweet Home" mingled with the crackle of the fire and the howl of some animal in the hills to their left.

"What's that?" Emmie knew her voice was too shrill when several of the soldiers snickered and Joel grinned.

"It's just a pack of coyotes," Isaac said. "They're more scared of you than you are of them."

Emmie shivered at another howl. "I wouldn't be too sure of that," she said shakily.

Rand played a couple of hymns and the men joined in song. Rooster had a surprisingly deep bass voice and Isaac sang tenor. But it had been a long day on the trail, and they were all yawning so Rand sent them all off to find their bedrolls twenty minutes later.

As Emmie crawled beneath her own blanket, she wondered about this life she found herself in. The unknown was so scary, but it was exhilarating, too. Was it perhaps her father's wanderlust blood coming to the fore? She'd always been content to stay close to hearth and home and had never dreamed she'd find herself in some wild land with rampaging coyotes and hostile savages. Maybe her father would finally be proud of her if he could see her now, she thought, snuggling deeper into the covers. Maybe he would even finally love her in spite of the fact that she wasn't a son. But to be honest, he hadn't had much use for Ben or Labe, either. All he'd ever cared about was his whiskey. He was long buried anyway, so there was no use in thinking about it. She would just concentrate on the future.

four

The landscape grew more wild and untamed as the procession turned north and trekked up toward Fort Phil Kearny. The mountains loomed in the distance, their purple peaks blending into the deep azure sky. Game flourished everywhere, and Rand had no trouble finding crack shots who could provide fresh meat to supplement the mess chest fare. The rest of the section he ordered to keep close together as they all kept a sharp lookout for Indians.

E. B. Taylor had attempted to negotiate a constructive peace treaty in May 1866, but Red Cloud had angrily stomped out when Colonel Carrington showed up to establish three new forts in the last of the Sioux hunting grounds. Red Cloud objected that the army would be setting up forts without waiting for the agreement from the Indians to allow troops to patrol the Bozeman Trail. These last three months had been tense, with numerous skirmishes between soldiers and Indians. Red Cloud was said to be massing together not just Sioux but Cheyenne and Arapaho to fight the invasion of bluecoats. Along this very trail just a month earlier, three soldiers had been killed and several others wounded during an ambush, Rand told them. So he preached constant vigilance and caution.

If the girls had been allowed to travel on horseback instead of riding the lurching ambulance, they would have enjoyed the trip immensely. As it was, they alternated between enduring the jolting ride and getting out and walking along the dusty trail. Emmie longed for a brief respite, just long enough to take a bath when they crossed a stream or occasionally glimpsed the Powder River.

The nights were cool and clear. Once Isaac pointed out a pack of timber wolves on a bluff overlooking the camp. He assured the girls they were safe from attack, but Emmie hadn't slept well that night. She dreamed of wolves surrounding her with red eyes and slavering fangs before being driven off by Isaac. He disturbed her dreams way too often.

Sarah worried her, too. Most mornings Emmie held the cracked tin bowl while Sarah was sick. By ten o'clock her friend was usually well enough to walk alongside the ambulance and laugh and joke with the men. But she grew paler and her laughter seemed forced by the fifth day.

"Have you noticed how poorly Sarah looks?" she asked Rand finally while Sarah was inside napping one afternoon.

He nodded, his brow crinkling with worry. "There's a post surgeon at Fort Phil Kearny. It's only another three days away or so. I just hope she can hold on. I've been thinking we might camp here an extra day. The horses could do with the rest, too."

"I think it might help if you thought it would be safe," she said. "She keeps pushing herself so. Today is the first time she's agreed to take a nap. A bath in the river might be nice, too."

Rand nodded slowly. "I'm anxious to get to the fort. The chance of meeting up with hostiles is pretty high, but I don't want Sarah to lose the baby. We'll just have to risk it. I'll post extra sentries and string up some blankets for privacy while you girls take a bath. I could use a bath and a shave myself." He rubbed his grizzled cheeks with a rueful grin.

A bath! Emmie almost skipped as she hurried to tell Sarah. Her friend was braiding her long red-gold hair when Emmie peeked in.

"You should have woken me," she said with a reproachful look. "I've been asleep for over two hours."

"You needed it. And guess what?" Emmie climbed in beside Sarah. "We're going to stop beside the creek for an extra day to rest up and bathe."

Sarah brightened immediately, a little pink rushing to her pale cheeks. "Oh, lovely. I was just feeling sorry for myself before you came. Missing home and Papa. Aren't I a silly goose?" She stood up as she thrust the last pin into place. "I'm so glad you're here, Emmie. I could not have endured this trip alone."

Emmie laughed self-consciously. "I'm just grateful I had somewhere to go when Monroe was killed." As she hugged her friend, she tried to push away the guilt she felt over not being completely honest. Someday the truth would have to be told, but not now. That was another good thing about being transferred to the remote fort. The mail hadn't been able to get through for over a month. With luck, by the time it did, everything would have died down in Indiana, and Margaret wouldn't mention her disgrace to Sarah.

The afternoon sun still blazed by the time they wandered down to the stream to find Rand, but the air was brisk. True to his word, he'd rigged up a rope with blankets around a lovely pool of water. The water looked clear and inviting, and Emmie couldn't wait to strip her clothes off and plunge in.

"I'll go get us some clean clothes," she told Sarah.

By the time she got back, Sarah had pulled off her shoes and stockings. She sat with her skirt pulled up to her knees and her feet dangling in the water. Emmie looked all around, but the soldiers were busy about their other duties setting up camp. Reassured of their privacy, she slipped behind the curtain and pulled off her stained and dusty dress and pulled the pins from her hair. She plunged in and came up sputtering. "It's like ice," she gasped.

Sarah wasted no time in joining her. Birds chirped in the trees around them and the breeze lapped the water into gentle waves and ripples as they quickly washed their hair. The water was too cold to stay long, and the air was chilly.

After they dressed, they left their hair down to dry as they washed their dirty clothes. Emmie thought Sarah looked better already. They spread their wet clothes out on the rocks and sat at the edge of the stream.

Emmie sighed, a sound of pure enjoyment as she felt the heat from the rock she was sitting on bake up through her chilled body. Almost dozing, she stretched out in the sun like a cat until a faint movement on the other side of the stream about fifty yards away caught her eye. "Oh, Sarah, look! Is that a buffalo?"

Sarah squinted against the glare of the sun as the movement came again. "Indians!" she screamed as she jumped to her feet.

Aware they'd been seen, the dim shapes rose to their feet and threw off their buffalo robes. Charging across the shallow creek with fierce yells, they headed straight toward the women with their tomahawks raised over their heads.

Emmie shrieked as she dashed toward the safety of the camp. She held tightly to Sarah's hand as they screamed for Rand.

Isaac and Rand, followed by four or five other soldiers, charged toward the Indians immediately. "Get under the wagon," Isaac ordered. Sarah grabbed Joel as he raced past them and dragged him under the wagon with them. Isaac dropped to one knee and aimed his rifle toward the advancing Indians. A fearsomely painted brave choked and fell seconds after the rifle cracked. Soldiers raced from all over the camp to join the fray. Emmie covered her ears at the booming gunfire and the terrifying screams and shouts. She was sure she and Sarah were about to die.

Rooster rolled in under the wagon beside the women. "Don't you fear, missy," he panted to Emmie. "No redskins gonna git ya. I'll shoot ya first myself 'fore I let them red devils take ya." Unaware of the shock his words caused Emmie, he fired his rifle methodically at the faltering horde of Sioux.

A few minutes later it was over. One man was dead and three were injured, including Rand, who had taken an arrow in the left arm.

"It's just a scratch," he said impatiently as Sarah fussed over him. "I'm all right, Green Eyes." He held her with his good arm as she burst into tears, then he saw Emmie's white face and held out his bleeding arm for her to join them. "Just what I've always wanted," he grinned when they finally regained their composure. "Two hysterical females watering my shirt."

Isaac's vivid blue eyes met Emmie's, and she had to check the impulse to run to him. Turning away from his anxious gaze, she pulled out of Rand's protective clasp so Sarah could tend to his wound. Emmie hurried toward the tent before she disgraced herself by begging Isaac to hold her. What was wrong with her anyway that she would have such a crazy thought? Men couldn't be trusted. She'd best not let herself forget that.

Three hours later, Emmie was still too keyed up to sleep. She could hear Rand's rhythmic breathing on the other side of the tent. Sarah snuffled occasionally in her sleep as she lay enfolded in Rand's good arm with Joel on the other side. She'd wanted to make sure both the males in her life were within arm's reach. Emmie shivered as she rolled over on her back and sat up. Maybe she'd just go out and sit by the fire for a while.

Rooster looked up as she lifted the flap on the tent and slipped outside. "Howdy, Miz Emmie. Can't sleep?"

She shook her head. "I've never been so frightened in my life, Rooster." She settled down beside him as he rummaged through his haversack and handed her a piece of jerky.

"Here. Jaw on this a while. It'll wear you out."

She smiled as she took the jerky. "Did you mean what you said about shooting us yourself?"

" 'Course I meant it. It's the unwritten law out here. We don't never want to let our wimmenfolk fall into the hands of them red devils. We know what they do to 'em. We been told to save a bullet for any female and one for ourselves."

Emmie shuddered. "What do they do to women?"

"Tain't no use in you knowin', cause it ain't going to happen to you." He avoided her eyes as he poked the fire with a stick.

"But what if it did?" she persisted. She always preferred to know the worst. It was one of her little quirks. And the things she imagined were always worse than the reality, so it was better to just know and set her mind at rest. Being killed by Indians couldn't be any worse in reality than it was in her imagination.

But Rooster just clamped his jaw tight. "Don't go coaxing me to tell you, 'cause I ain't gonna do it. Old Rooster ain't never goin' to let them red devils git you, so don't you bother yer purty head about it."

And that's all he would say, so Emmie had to be content with the horrors of her imagination. She could tell he meant what he said about shooting her himself first, too. And that scared her. What if one of the soldiers shot them because they thought they'd be captured and help arrived just in the nick of time or something? She shivered. Maybe she should ask Rand to change the rule. She yawned, finally sleepy, and mumbling goodnight to Rooster, made her way back to her tent.

The next morning Sarah looked much better. Rand had awakened them early and was even more eager to reach the safe haven of Fort Phil Kearny after the ambush the day before. As they rolled along, Isaac rode next to the ambulance and pointed out the majestic peaks in the distance.

"That's the Bighorn Mountains. Beautiful, aren't they? This Powder River country is the last of the Sioux hunting grounds. It's usually thick with buffalo, but they're already beginning to thin out from the white man hunting them. The Indians are afraid if they let us establish the Bozeman Trail along here that we'll drive away the last of the game. And they're right, as usual. It's already beginning to happen."

Emmie looked at Isaac's face, bright with awe and love for the land. His nose was peeling a bit from the sun and his blue eyes stood out in sharp contrast to his tanned face. He seemed so solid and dependable mounted on his horse. She felt a tugging at her heartstrings and looked away.

Later that night, Emmie mentioned what Isaac had said. After the terror of the day before, Emmie thought it might be a good thing for the game to be driven away. Maybe the Indians would decide to be civilized if they couldn't find game.

"I lived with the Sioux for a short while, you know," Sarah said. "It was a curiously peaceful life where we worked for our food and really lacked nothing important. Their ways aren't any different to us than our ways are to the Europeans. The Indian women do beautiful needlework. Sometime I'll show you my buckskin dress and let you see inside a Sioux tepee. My friend, White Beaver, taught me a lot about what's really important in life. Things like love and unity and self-sufficiency. You would like her."

"Where is she now?"

"With Little Wolverine in Red Cloud's resistance, as far as I know. Rand and I tried to talk them out of going, but they said they had to stand with their people before the Sioux are no more."

Emmie could tell Sarah really respected her Indian friends and it surprised her. "How can Rand fight the Indians when he has friends among them? What if Little Wolverine were with the band who attacked?"

"It would be Rand's worst nightmare to have to fight his friend. I don't know if he could or not. But Wolverine said they would always be friends, so I don't think he would ever attack us."

Their discussion was interrupted by shouts from the front of the procession. "Phil Kearny ahead!"

Sarah and Emmie both thrust their heads out under the rolled-up canvas on the sides of the wagon and looked eagerly for their destination. Emmie could see sentries on a hill ahead waving signal flags.

"They're signaling our arrival to the fort," Sarah told her. "The commander will send out an escort."

Rand had ordered the women to stay in the ambulance away from the possible eyes of hostiles, but Emmie longed to climb out of the lurching conveyance and run on ahead to the fort. The thought of sleeping in a real bed was enticing. As she and Sarah looked toward the fort, a wagon loaded with wood lumbered by. On the back of the wagon a bloodstained figure lolled, one arm flung down the back of the wagon. Emmie thought he looked like he had red hair like Isaac until Sarah gasped.

"That soldier's been scalped," Sarah choked out, her hand to her mouth.

Emmie shuddered and looked around fearfully for the Indians who had committed the atrocity. But the wooded hills around the fort looked peaceful. The ambulance jerked forward as the driver urged the horses to a trot. Rand had seen the dead soldier and motioned the troops to hurry toward the safety of the fort.

As they pulled inside the stockaded garrison, soldiers milled around shouting orders. "Do you see Amelia?" Sarah asked anxiously.

Emmie looked around but saw no other women. "It's around lunch time," she said, consulting her gold watch pinned to her dress. "Maybe we could find her in the mess hall."

They climbed down out of the ambulance. Emmie was glad to be on solid ground again. She felt a little unsteady on her feet as though the ground was lurching under her. She looked around the tiny fort. "It looks more like I thought Laramie would look," she said. "There are stockades and sentries along the block houses."

Sarah nodded. "If that murdered soldier is anything to go by, they need all the protection they can get. There's no telegraph line strung this far north, so if they've been having a lot of trouble with hostiles, they wouldn't be able to wire for reinforcements." Joel was dancing around impatiently, so she gave him permission to go look for his friend.

Rand stepped up and put an arm around Sarah. "I'll see if I can find Jake and Amelia. You look done in. While you're resting at Amelia's, I'll see the quartermaster and get our housing assignment." But before he could go look for his brother, he heard a familiar voice.

"Rand!" His brother Jake ran toward them and seconds later the brothers were hugging and slapping one another on the back. "I can't believe you're here. And Sarah, too. Amelia will be ecstatic. She's been driving me crazy with missing Sarah." He pulled Sarah into a bear hug, then his handsome face sobered when he saw Emmie. Rand gave him one last clap on the back and hurried off to find the quartermaster.

Emmie knew Rand's brother Jacob—or Jake as everyone called him—had never liked Ben. She hadn't had much occasion to talk to Jake herself, so she assumed his reserve was because of her brother. He would just have to find out she wasn't like her brother. She held out her hand. "Hello, Jake."

He smiled then and took her hand. "Emmie. What are you doing here? Did your husband join the army? Ma wrote when you got married."

Sarah rushed in as she saw Emmie bite her lip. "Emmie's a widow and she's here to keep me company. But there's plenty of time for explanations later. I'm dying to see Amelia. Where is she?"

"I'll show you to our quarters. She's been feeling poorly, and I told her to rest this afternoon."

"What's wrong with her?" Sarah's voice was alarmed as she and Emmie hurried to keep up with Jake's long strides as he led them across the uncompleted parade ground toward a row of wooden houses.

He grinned. "You'll have to ask her."

"You don't mean—"

"Yeah. Can you believe I'm going to be a papa? Rand and I are going to make each other uncles within a few weeks of one another."

Sarah clapped her hands together. "Wait until Rand hears!"

"Here we are." He stopped beside a small wooden house.

Emmie looked around curiously. The home was tiny, and sap ran from the cuts and nicks in the logs. She touched a sticky lump. It smelled like pine. She'd noticed coming toward the fort that this area had a lot more trees than down around Laramie.

Jake pushed open the door and led them into a tiny parlor with a fireplace in one wall. It looked much like the home they'd left except it was even smaller. "It doesn't look like much now, I know," he said with an apologetic grin. "I haven't had time to knock together a table and chairs for the kitchen yet, so we've been eating in the parlor. It's pretty inconvenient for Amelia, but I told her I'd make sure I got to it this week. The Indians have been a constant nuisance. Even the wood detail has to be accompanied by armed troops. And that doesn't always stop Red Cloud's band, as I'm sure you noticed on the way in."

"Who was the murdered soldier?" Sarah asked as Jake led the way through the minuscule kitchen toward the closed door on the far side. "Did I know him?"

"No, he was a new recruit. Corporal Johnson was his name and he was as hotheaded as they come. We're just lucky more weren't killed. Some of the men have been spoiling for a fight, but I thank the good Lord that Carrington has been able to restrain them so far." He pushed open the door to the bedroom and smiled when he saw his wife.

She lay on her side, one arm outflung and her face pink in sleep. Her black hair was unbound and fanned out on the pillow in a silken cloud. Emmie saw Jake's face soften in love and pride as he gazed at his sleeping wife.

"Honey. Look who's here." He spoke gently as he took her hand.

Her long lashes fluttered and she opened her eyes blearily. She stared for a long minute into Sarah's eyes, then bolted upright. "Sarah?" She looked over at Jake, then back at Sarah.

Sarah bounded forward and jumped onto the bed. "It's me, Amelia. It's really me."

Jealousy, scalding and acrid, overwhelmed Emmie as she saw Sarah and Amelia fall into one another's arms with tears of joy. She'd always liked Amelia, but she'd grown to regard

Sarah as her best friend over the past weeks. Bleakly, she knew she would have to settle for second place in Sarah's affections. Unconsciously, she squared her shoulders and pushed the hurt feelings away. She would not be like her brother Ben. He had allowed jealousy and possessiveness to ruin his life and Labe's, too. She'd come here alone and she could leave the same way if she had to. But she admitted to herself that she didn't want to leave. It felt grand to laugh with friends like Sarah and Rand.

Amelia drew away and noticed Emmie standing unobtrusively to one side. "Why, dear Emmie, too!" She slipped out of the bed and ran to give her a quick hug. "How wonderful to see you. I had no idea you were with Sarah. Is Monroe with you?"

Amelia seemed truly glad to see her, Emmie thought. She shook her head at Amelia's question. She glanced gratefully at Sarah, who rushed in with a quick explanation of Emmie's circumstances.

"You poor dear," Amelia said with another quick hug. "No wonder you look so peaked. I am glad you're here, though you may want to run screaming for home with two crotchety women in delicate condition for company."

"Well, I'll leave you three to get caught up on all the gossip and go find my brother," Jake put in.

The girls barely noticed his departure as they all three piled on the bed and began to talk at once. "We brought some fresh newspapers from back east with us—they're only two months old," Sarah said.

"And I brought a magazine of new fashions Margaret sent with me. I've been saving it until winter settled in, but we could get it out whenever you want," Emmie added.

"Let's save it until we can get together with the other ladies," Amelia said. "You'll love our little community. There's Mrs. Horton, the wife of our post surgeon and Surgeon in Chief of the Mountain District; Mrs. Carrington, the commander's wife; Mrs. Wands; Mrs. Bisbee; and Mrs. Grummond. They've been a wonderful help to me." She slipped off the bed, and picking up the hairbrush from the barrel that served as a nightstand, began to put her hair up. "Let's have some tea and then I'll introduce you to the ladies."

five

The bugle sounded retreat as Isaac strode through Fort Phil Kearny. The fort bustled with activity as soldiers led their horses toward the stables and hurried to get ready for evening mess. Isaac thought he'd never seen a more beautiful spot than this Tongue River Valley. The Bighorn Mountains south of the valley, the Panther Mountains to the west, and the Black Hills to the east all formed a majestic backdrop to this busy little fort in the wilderness. Black-billed magpies scrabbled in the thin dirt in search of food, while flocks of mountain chickadees chirped in the trees outside the fort. The smell of cut pine and sawdust mingled with the scent of horse and wood smoke as he made his way through the tradesman encampment. The air was fresh with the scent of imminent rain, and Isaac could see thunderheads towering like newly forming mountains to the west.

The stockade was not yet completely finished. Its walls of hewn pine were interspersed with block guardhouses situated diagonally at the corners of the fort, and the gates were made of massive double planks with small sally wickets and a small sally port for the officers' use. Immediately inside was the quartermaster's yard, a cottonwood corral that housed the teamsters and their stock along with wagons, hayricks, and the shops for wagon makers and leather workers. Just beyond that was the fort proper with officers' row, the barracks, and the sutler's store. He skirted the manure and mud as he hurried toward the Campbell quarters.

Emmie opened the door when he knocked. He grinned at the startled look on her face.

"Isaac. I thought it was Rand." A delicate blush bloomed in her cheeks, and she avoided his eyes.

47

"He sent me to fetch you two ladies. Your quarters are ready for your inspection." He took out his large, white handkerchief and carefully wiped the corner of her mouth. "Jam," he said with a gentle smile. He wished he could kiss it off.

Emmie flushed. Why did he always have to catch her at such a disadvantage? Besides, she wasn't interested in a flirtation with anyone, no matter how attractive. He looked particularly handsome with his auburn hair ruffled by the wind and his face tanned from the sun. Her face flamed a deeper hue as he grinned at her discomfiture. "I'll get Sarah," she said abruptly. She left him standing at the open door as she went to fetch her friend.

"Are our quarters close to Amelia?" Sarah asked. She and Emmie snatched up their bonnets from the hook near the door and followed Isaac down the steps.

"The permanent ones will be next door."

"Permanent ones? Where are we going now?"

Isaac pointed toward a group of tents in a small open space near the quartermaster's yard.

"You're joking, right?" Sarah stopped and looked up at Isaac in dismay. "Amelia says we'll have snow soon. We can't live in a tent."

"It's just while your quarters are built. We've put a Sibley stove in for you to keep the cold away. He tried his best to get you something else. Jake even offered to let you stay with them, but you saw how small their place is. This is the best the quartermaster could do on short notice."

Sarah caught the warning tone in Isaac's voice and bit her lip. "Well, if it's the best he could do, then we have no choice. Please don't say anything to Rand about my being upset," she said.

Isaac smiled his approval. "Good girl." He glanced at Emmie. "Think you can stand it, too?"

"Of course," she said with more certainty than she felt.

He smiled again, and Emmie thought she saw a hint of admiration in his blue eyes, but she pushed the thought away.

She didn't want admiration or anything else from him, she told herself firmly. Not from him or any other man.

Rand was busy directing soldiers where to put the barrels of their belongings when they arrived. "I'm sorry, Green Eyes, but this will have to do for now. But it's not too bad. See, we've put three A tents together to make three rooms. We can store our trunks and mess chest in one. You and I can sleep in here, and Emmie can have the next one. Joel is going to stay with the Carringtons until our quarters are ready. There's a stove in Emmie's room, too, as well as this one. Will you be all right?"

"Of course. This is very pleasant, Rand." Sarah walked through the interconnected tents with Emmie following close behind. Two army cots and the stove took up most of the room in the Campbells' room, but Emmie would have a bit more floor space for possessions.

"We could use my room as a parlor during the day," Emmie said with a quick look around. She was very conscious of Isaac's nearness as he hovered at her elbow. When he looked at her, she felt as though he was looking into her very soul.

"You'll probably spend most of your daylight hours with Amelia and the other ladies," Rand said. "But thanks for the offer."

Sarah and Emmie covered their dismay about their quarters with nervous chatter about the fort and questioned Rand about what he'd learned of the situation.

"I really wish I hadn't brought you both here," he admitted. "Jake says no one is allowed outside the fort except for fighting and absolute necessities. Troops escort wagon trains occasionally, but Amelia hasn't been outside the stockade in two months. Red Cloud's tactics seem to be constant harassment. There's some kind of skirmish almost every day, and the Indians seem to be getting bolder in their ploys."

"But Amelia said some of the ladies even brought their children with them. It surely can't be that dangerous."

"I think Carrington and headquarters had no idea how

strongly the Sioux would object to this fort. They call this harassment the 'Circle of Death.' Jake says they're determined to drive the whites from here for good."

The bugle sounded mess call and Rand took Sarah's arm. "What's done is done now," he said, steering her toward the officers' mess hall. "But I want you both to stay away from the stockade walls, and if you're told to get to safety, obey immediately."

Isaac took Emmie's arm and escorted her to the mess hall. She could feel the smooth muscles of his forearm under his coat sleeve, and she wanted to draw her hand away. To do so would have been rude, though, and it wasn't Isaac's fault that she found him entirely too attractive for her own peace of mind.

By the time they ate the luncheon of ever-present salt pork and beans, reconstituted vegetables, and coffee, the first fat drops of rain had begun to fall. The clouds obscured the sun and cast a dark pall over the fort as the wind howled like a thousand banshees. The men had already left for their afternoon duties, and Emmie glanced at the sky nervously as she and Sarah left the mess hall. They ran for the safety of Amelia's quarters, with the wind driving sand and cold rain into their skin like a horde of vicious mosquitoes. Soaked and chilled, they burst through the door into Amelia's parlor. As they shook the water out of their clothes and hair, a horrendous pounding and clattering began all around them.

"What is it?" Emmie cried. She'd been terrified of storms ever since she'd been caught in the field during an Indiana thunderstorm once, cowering in terror in a ditch while a blackish-green tornado had whirled above her.

They all ran to the front window and looked out on a scene of utter pandemonium. Horses reared in terror and soldiers fought to control them as man and beast alike were pelted with hail the size of eggs. The white missiles fell so hard they left dents in the soft ground. Emmie saw several soldiers cringe beneath the blows as their hats went flying. It only lasted for a few minutes, but by the time the freakish weather was over, the post surgeon had several bleeding soldiers to attend to. One man was trampled beneath the hooves of a panicked horse. The three women worried about the men until Amelia spied her husband under the overhanging roof of the sutler's store. He waved at them cheerily and gave no evidence of dismay, so they assumed everyone was all right.

❧

The next morning Emmie awoke with something tickling her nose. She could hear the wind howling through the tent, but she had piled on so many blankets and buffalo robes, she was pleasantly warm and comfortable. She reached up to scratch her nose and touched cold, dry snow. During the night the early snowstorm had arrived, and the wind blew the powdery fluff through the cracks in the tent openings. A thick layer of white stuff covered Emmie and all her possessions.

She sat up and shook the snow from her hair and bedclothes. Scrambling out of bed, she emptied the snow from her shoes. She felt oddly lightheaded as she shook her dress thoroughly and pulled her nightgown over her head. By the time she was dressed, she was shivering almost uncontrollably. As she bent over to tie her boots, she almost tumbled to the floor as a wave of dizziness washed over her. Straightening up, she retched with a suddenly overwhelming attack of nausea. She hurriedly reached for the chamber pot at the end of her cot and vomited into it. What on earth was wrong with her? She couldn't get sick now, she thought frantically as she sank back on the bunk, clutching the chamber pot weakly. Not with Sarah and Amelia dependent on her. They both felt poorly so often; who would clean up and cook if she fell ill?

As she thought of their condition, a terrible thought assailed her. When did she have her last monthly? Another wave of nausea shook her as she lay weakly back against the pillow and thought about it. She hadn't had her monthly at all in August, and September's should have arrived last week. She closed her eyes as she contemplated the possibility that she might be pregnant. It could be, couldn't it? Weak tears trickled from beneath her closed eyes. Was there no end to her shame? Did she now have to bear a bastard child? Surely not. This was probably just a result of being chilled in the night—or perhaps the influenza, or maybe even cholera. Anything, even something deadly, would be preferable to what she suspected was true.

Sarah had evidently heard her retching for she scratched at the opening between the two tents. "Emmie? Are you all right? I'm coming in." She didn't wait for an answer but pushed open the flap and entered. She hurried straight to the bed where Emmie lay bleakly contemplating how much to tell her friend.

"I'm fine. Just a little sick feeling. It's probably nothing."

Sarah's practiced eye took in her friend's pallor and the whiteness around her mouth. "Rand, please ask Dr. Horton to stop by," she called to her husband, who hovered near the doorway. "I don't like the way she looks. And get the fire going in the stove, too, please." She turned briskly back to Emmie. "Now I want you to get back in your nightgown and into bed. It's my turn to take care of you."

"I'm feeling much better. Maybe if I had a cracker and some tea—," Emmie stammered.

"The very thing. That always helps me when I feel sick. I'll be right back with some, and I want to find you snuggled in the covers when I return." With a last admonishing wag of her finger, Sarah stepped through the tent flap.

Wearily Emmie pulled off her clothes and tugged on her thick flannel nightgown. There was no use in protesting. Little Sarah could be implacable when she thought she was in the right.

Sarah returned with the steaming tea and a tin of crackers at the same time Dr. Horton arrived with his black bag. He was a tall, spare man in his forties, with a balding pate and a pleasant smile and demeanor. "Well, now, what seems to be the matter, young lady? You should be up and about. That pretty face of yours is good for morale." He set his bag down on the bed and drew out his stethoscope. Rand came in just behind him and began to poke at the coals in the stove.

Sarah handed the tea and crackers to Emmie. "I'll run over and get Amelia while the doctor's with you."

"There's really no need—" But Sarah was gone before Emmie could finish her protest. Rand followed her out after winking at Emmie kindly.

"When did you start feeling poorly?" the doctor asked, putting the cold stethoscope against her chest.

"Just this morning." She bent forward obediently as he placed the stethoscope on her back and listened intently. She answered the rest of his questions and lay back against the pillow as he probed around on her stomach.

"Ah," he said after a few moments.

"What is it?"

"When did you have your last monthly?"

Oh no. She swallowed hard, then told him in a hoarse whisper.

He nodded. "I'd say you're increasing. The little one should arrive about mid-May." He frowned when he noticed her obvious distress. "You don't seem overjoyed."

"My husband is dead, Dr. Horton, and I have no family."

He nodded again. "Yes, I know. But, at least you're among friends. And I'm sure in a fort full of eligible men you could find a father for your baby if you wished."

"I'm not interested in marrying again," she whispered. The doctor raised his eyebrows at her answer, and she laid a hand on his arm. "You've been very kind. How long will the morning sickness last?"

"Hard to say." He stood and began to put his things back in his bag. "It could only be for a few weeks or a few months. If you're really unlucky, it could last your entire pregnancy. But most women find it subsides after four or five weeks." He gestured at the crackers in her hand. "Those usually help if you keep some beside your bed and nibble on them before you even get out of bed. I would suggest you stay in bed today—you've had quite a shock, and I can see it's upset you. If you need me again, just send one of the men for me." He patted her hand kindly. "At least you won't be alone any longer. God knows best, my dear." With a final pat he hurried away.

Emmie closed her eyes and a few tears slipped out from under her lashes. It was easy for him to say that God knew best. He wasn't alone in the world. She had no means of supporting herself, let alone a baby. What was she going to do? Rand and Sarah wouldn't throw her out, but she was supposed to be here to help Sarah, not be an additional burden on her friends who'd been so kind. She had no skills, no resources. She shuddered from the hopelessness of her situation. Why did she ever have to meet Monroe? Her life was in ruins.

She turned her head as Sarah and Amelia hurried into her tent. Amelia looked as anxious as Sarah did, and Emmie felt a wave of love for both friends. They truly did care about her. She didn't know why they should, but they did, and she was grateful to both of them.

"What did the doctor say?" Sarah laid a cool hand on Emmie's forehead.

Emmie bit her lip. There was no use trying to keep it from them. "I'm going to have a baby."

Sarah's eyes widened, and she gaped before she recovered her composure. "Oh, Emmie, that's wonderful! When?"

"May."

Amelia clapped her hands in delight. "It will be such fun for us to raise our babies together. We'll have all kinds of good advice for you by the time the wee one arrives."

Emmie was grateful for the way they were hiding the dismay they must both be feeling. "I'll be fine in a day or two, and I promise not to be a bother, Sarah. I'm supposed to be helping you."

"Oh, pish posh, I don't need any help. I just needed company. You'll be even better company now that you know what we're going through."

"But what will Rand say?"

"What do you mean?" Sarah seemed genuinely puzzled. "What could he say? He loves kids." She fluffed up Emmie's pillow and pushed her down against it. "Now you just quit your fretting and get some rest. Everything is going to be just fine. You'll see."

Emmie allowed herself to be tucked into the quilts and furs as the fire in the stove threw out welcome warmth and cheeriness. She didn't know what the future might hold, but with friends like the Campbells, it would surely be all right.

six

Indeed, Emmie found that Rand treated her no differently than he always had over the days that followed. He was just as solicitous of her as he was Sarah. He truly did not seem to mind the change in the bargain they'd struck, and Emmie began to relax. She was not sure if Rand told Isaac, but he didn't stop by as often as before. As the days passed and the chilly October wind blew while the fort prepared for winter, she told herself she didn't care if he came by or not. All men were fickle at best and treacherous at worst.

Early one sunny day in late October, Rand announced their permanent quarters were ready to move into. Several soldiers showed up eager to be of service, and they soon had their few possessions hoisted on their shoulders and hauled across the parade ground to the three-room quarters. It was similar to what they'd left behind in Fort Laramie in layout but smaller in size. The fresh-cut pine boards still oozed sap and smelled of newly milled lumber. The fresh plaster walls looked clean but stark, with no trim around the windows or floor. The kitchen was bare of accessories but serviceable and clean. Emmie was so glad to be out of the tent, she didn't care how it looked.

"It's plain, I know, but I'll knock together a dry sink and corner cupboard as soon as I can," Rand said apologetically.

"Already done, partner," Isaac's voice broke in. He grinned as he set a sturdy sawhorse down against the wall. "Be right back." He stepped outside and came right back in with another one, which he placed a couple of feet away from the first. Then he brought in four rough planks of wood and laid them over the sawhorses. "This is the very latest in Fort Phil's kitchen decor. All the best-dressed kitchens have one. And I have it on the best authority that it makes a dandy ironing board as well."

"Isaac, you darling!" Sarah exclaimed. She ran to hug him.

"Don't I get a hug from you, too?" he asked Emmie with a grin.

Emmie felt the warm blood rush to her cheeks. He hadn't shown his face for days and now he showed up talking about hugs. "Maybe when we get the chairs," she said awkwardly. She flushed again when he laughed. What a stupid thing to say, she told herself disgustedly. But he'd caught her off guard.

"I'll hold you to it," he chuckled as he walked away.

Emmie was amazed how easily she and Sarah adapted to their rough surroundings. She'd never had nice things growing up, but Monroe had insisted on the finest of everything, and she had found herself enjoying every luxury. Now she was content with the barest necessities.

They delighted in fixing up their tiny home over the next few days. They begged some wool blankets from the quartermaster and tacked them together to make rugs for the parlor and bedroom floors as well as for the small area in the hall that was partitioned off for Emmie. Rand came in with a triumphant smile one afternoon with his booty of blue gingham for curtains and tablecloths. With Sarah's little knickknacks around, the place looked very homey. Several of the other ladies were very friendly and stopped by with invitations to tea and some small offerings of household items.

"I think I'll go for a walk," Emmie told Sarah one evening after the supper dishes were done. Rand had taken Joel and gone out to make some rounds, and things were just too quiet for Emmie. She didn't like having too much time to think. "The wind isn't blowing too hard for a change. I'm going crazy cooped up inside. Want to come along?"

"I don't think so. Rand tore his britches on some cactus yesterday, and I promised I'd mend them. Why don't you ask Isaac or one of the other officers to escort you? Any of them would jump at the chance."

"No thanks. I don't mind going alone." Emmie shied away from the thought of Isaac. She had tried to avoid him ever since he brought by the camp chairs for the kitchen while she was taking their laundry to Soapsuds Row two days ago. *He's surely forgotten all about that stupid remark I made,* she told herself.

The cool night air felt invigorating, but Emmie shivered as wolves howled outside the stockade. She wrapped her cloak more tightly around her as she strolled along the sawdust path in front of the officers' quarters. She decided to wander in the direction of the front of the stockade.

"Mind if I join you?" A tall shadow came toward her, and she flinched back before she recognized Isaac's smiling face.

"There's really no need. I'm perfectly all right. I just wanted a walk." Her pulse quickened and she took a step back.

"I could use a chance to stretch my legs myself." He fell into step beside her. "Did you have someplace special in mind to go or shall we just look in some windows?"

She chuckled in spite of herself, then glanced at him hesitantly. He probably wouldn't let her do what she planned. "I know Rand said to stay away from the stockade perimeter, but I wish I could climb up in the blockhouse and look out over the wall for just a minute. I'm so tired of seeing the same things day after day. I haven't been outside the confines of this fort in weeks."

Isaac was silent for a minute. She shivered again as she heard a pack of wolves howl off to her right, but Isaac relaxed at the sound. "Those are real wolves and not Indians. I guess it wouldn't hurt for just a minute. But you have to promise to get away from the wall the minute I say we have to leave."

"I promise," she said excitedly. He was really going to take her!

Isaac led her past the hospital and warehouses and through the tangle of hayricks and shops and quarters for wagon makers and saddlers. He stepped carefully and pointed out piles of manure and mud for her to avoid before stopping outside the blockhouse. "Let me tell the soldiers on duty what we're doing," he said. He disappeared inside the door and returned several moments later with a smile on his face.

"What's so funny?"

"I told Corporal Lengel I wanted to show you the moon on the Little Piney River."

"He'll think—"

"Well, I had to give him some reason."

Emmie flushed as she followed Isaac's broad back up the ladder. She didn't want anyone getting the wrong idea about her and Isaac. Rumors could run through their little community like a herd of thundering buffalo. The corporal grinned knowingly as they brushed past him to get to the window.

"Call when you're finished here, Captain," he said, his grin widening as he backed down the ladder.

"Now see what you've done," Emmie said. She was glad it was too dark for Isaac to see her hot cheeks.

Isaac just laughed. Ignoring her outburst, he pointed out the window. "Look at the river."

Emmie looked and caught her breath. The trees along the river looked as though they were made of diamonds. The moon glittered on their coating of heavy frost and the iced-over river caught the shimmering reflection and bounced it back. She longed to run out and skate along its shining surface. She leaned out the window, but Isaac caught her arm and pulled her back.

"Don't do that! There could be Sioux out there just waiting to put an arrow through your pretty head."

Emmie swallowed hard and shrank back against his side. A warning bell rang inside her head as she realized how close he was. She straightened up and started to pull away, but he caught her and turned her to face him.

"A real lady always pays her debts, you know."

"What do you mean?" Her heart thundered in her ears. She knew what he intended and put up one hand against his chest.

She could feel the thud of his heart under her fingers. She knew she should run as fast as she could, but his warm male scent was intoxicating.

His voice was husky as he leaned closer. "I distinctly remember you promising me a hug when I brought the kitchen chairs. It's been two days and I haven't gotten my hug yet. I think I'd better charge you a little interest."

He gathered her closer. Emmie stared mesmerized as he bent his head. She smelled the warm scent of his skin as his lips found hers, and she found herself responding in spite of her resolve. His kiss was gentle at first but began to turn into something else as she finally gathered her strength and pulled away.

"That was more than a little interest!" She was trembling in spite of the warmth of her cloak.

"I think it was just perfect." He traced a finger along the curve of her cheek. "Just like you."

"I–I'd better get back." She swallowed hard. "Sarah will be wondering about me."

He nodded and let her go. She kept a wary eye on him as she took one last look out the window, then hurried down the ladder. She didn't wait for him but struck off toward the officers' quarters.

"Wait up, Emmie. What are you so scared of? I won't hurt you."

"I–I don't want you to think I'm the sort of girl who dallies in the moonlight," she gulped, her voice nearly inaudible. "Just because I'm a widow doesn't mean I'm looking for someone to fill in for Monroe."

"I never thought you were." Isaac's voice was cold. "That husband of yours must have been a piece of work for you to be so prickly, but you don't need to lump all of us men in the same pot of stew. I wouldn't want to do anything to dishonor you or my God."

"Don't you say anything about Monroe! You don't know anything about him." She was near tears. Isaac's mention of dishonor flooded her with shame and guilt. She'd had all she could bear of the soaring heights of love; she knew all too well how hard the blow was when the time came to come back to earth.

"I know he must have hurt you badly. When you arrived at Fort Laramie, you were like a stray dog everyone had kicked too often. I left you alone to lick your wounds, but it's time for you to put the past behind you and get on with your life." He swept his arm expansively. "This is a new country out here. You can forget Indiana. God sent you out here to make a new life for yourself. Don't throw His gift back in His face."

"I am making a new life. It just doesn't include kisses in the moonlight with you or anyone else," Emmie said softly, near tears. His tender kiss had awakened feelings she didn't want stirred.

"Maybe I'm rushing you a little," Isaac said. He stepped back away from her. "But I'll be here when you decide to quit living in the past." He turned and strode back toward the officers' quarters.

Emmie's throat burned with unshed tears as she mounted the steps to the door. *I just don't want to be hurt again,* she thought, trying to compose herself. *He's only interested because there aren't any other unmarried women here,* she told herself firmly. *If we were in Indiana, he wouldn't give me a second glance.* She'd never felt she was a lovable person until Monroe came into her life. And after he'd done what he did, she was sure there was something inherently wrong with her. No one had ever loved her for herself. Not even her family.

Sarah looked up as she came in. "Did you have a nice walk? Oh—" She broke off when she saw the look on Emmie's face. "What's wrong?"

"Nothing. I'm just tired." Emmie forced a smile to her face. She felt Sarah's probing eyes, but she refused to meet her gaze. "I think I'll turn in early. I'll see you in the morning." She fled to the meager haven of her curtained-off bedroom.

Sarah wouldn't understand, she told herself. She'd like to see her marry Isaac and settle down next door. But that wasn't going to happen, she vowed as she slipped between the cold sheets. Men just couldn't be trusted. Under his exuberance and flattery, Monroe had been just like her brothers and father. Just as selfish and deceitful. Isaac was no different. He was just hiding it like Monroe had done. Monroe's kisses had seemed tender and loving, too.

The next morning was Sunday. Emmie hummed as she donned her best dress and pulled her raven hair back in a ribbon. She'd managed to vanquish thoughts of Isaac in the night and was determined not to let him unsettle her. A church service would actually be held in the little post chapel today. A chaplain had arrived earlier in the week and would lead the little post's first service.

She'd never attended church in Wabash other than an occasional wedding. Her pa didn't hold with religion, even though he bellowed out hymns when he was drunk. Emmie always wondered where he'd learned them. He never talked much about how he was raised and she never knew her grandparents. Her pa always said religion was a crutch for weak people, but personally, Emmie thought the liquor was more of a crutch. She wanted to know more about what made her friends so different. Maybe it was their religion. Church should be interesting.

Sarah looked at her sharply as she pushed the curtain back and stepped into the parlor. "You seem in a fine mood today."

"It's a beautiful morning for a church service," Emmie said. "I've never been to a real church service. Only weddings."

"Rand is so disappointed to miss it. He has orders to lead a squad to guard the wood detail. I promised to tell him all about it tonight."

The chapel was a small cabin with seats that were rough backless benches oozing sap. A small stove in one corner of the room belched out smoke along with a little warmth. Emmie, Sarah, and Joel sat on the second row beside Amelia.

The chaplain, Reverend Howard, was a nervous young man with thin, pale hair and a straggly mustache. He read from Isaiah 43:1–2: " 'Fear not: for I have redeemed thee, I have called thee by thy name; thou art mine. When thou passest through the waters, I will be with thee; and through the rivers, they shall not overflow thee: when thou walkest through the fire, thou shalt not be burned; neither shall the flame kindle upon thee.' " He closed his large Bible and cleared his throat. "Though it seems we are compassed about by the enemy in this place, God tells us to fear not. He is with us and He will be our shield and comfort."

Although he stammered occasionally as he spoke of God's protection, Emmie was drawn by the words. Was the minister right? And Isaac? She glanced at the back of his head in the row in front of her. He leaned slightly forward in his seat as he listened intently. Did God really care about her in a personal way? She'd never doubted the existence of God, but in her mind, He was a powerful being who looked down on mere mortals with distant interest. Oh, He might deign to involve Himself in the moving of nations and history, but He wasn't concerned with the small day-to-day heartbreaks of an ordinary person like her. But was He? Did He send her out here to such good friends as the Campbells because He loved her and cared for her? The thought was comforting, and she wished she could believe it. It would be nice to be able to rest in His protection like the minister said. Emmie sighed. She'd have to think about it.

As the service ended and they stood to leave, Isaac's eyes caught hers for just a moment. She looked away quickly as Frances Grummond called to them. She was glad for an excuse to turn away from Isaac's warm eyes. The look in his gaze threatened to upset all her carefully laid plans to keep her distance.

"Yoo hoo, Emmie." Frances waved at them from across the room. She was a petite brunette with softly rounded curves and a delightful southern accent. She, too, was expecting a baby soon. She hurried over when she saw she had her attention. "I'm having tea at my house. Won't you all join me?"

Sarah smiled and clapped her hands. "The very thing! I've gotten so tired of those same four walls. What can I bring?"

"I have everything prepared. I know my lack of cooking prowess is legendary, but my husband has secured the services of Private Brown as cook. His scones are exemplary."

"Sounds lovely," Amelia said with a gentle smile. "Our men are out on wood detail or guard duty. What time do you want us?"

"Oh, about three. Bring your mending or whatever and we'll have a fine time of chatting. Mrs. Horton is joining us, also."

The three thanked her again and hurried toward home, after waving good-bye to Joel, who went off quite happily with his friend, Jimmy Carrington. The fierce October wind whipped their cloaks about as they fought to keep their balance in the gale. Emmie had to keep a hand on her hat to prevent it from blowing away. Sometimes she thought she'd go mad from the wind. It never seemed to stop. Not even in the summer, Sarah said.

The fire was almost out as they stepped inside Amelia's quarters. "I'll get the fire going," Emmie said. The wind blew down the chimney and sent ashes flying all over her and into the room as she opened the stove door. She quickly threw two logs in and shut the door again.

"Let's just have some soup, since we'll be having tea with Frances," Sarah said. "I'm really not that hungry, are you?"

"Not at all," Emmie said. "Soup would be lovely. I'll warm it up." She opened the back door and lifted the brick off the pan sitting on the ground. There were too many roving dogs to set the pan out without something heavy on the lid. She put the pan on the stove and turned to tie on an apron before she soiled her dress.

"I feel sorry for poor Frances," Amelia said.

"She seems happy enough," Emmie said. "Why should you feel sorry for her?"

"Her husband doesn't seem to give her much thought. He's always out playing poker at the sutler's store or trying to stir up some of the men to go on some confrontation with the Indians. Mrs. Horton says this is his second marriage. I have a feeling it won't be long before Lieutenant Grummond's hot blood brings him in harm's way. And poor little Frances is so loyal and sweet."

"But aren't most men a lot like that?" Emmie asked as she stirred the soup. "My brothers were, and so was Monroe."

Sarah and Amelia shared a long look.

"Rand and Jake are different, of course," Emmie said hastily. "But you two are luckier than most."

"Actually, Emmie, I'm glad you brought this up," Sarah said slowly. "I've wanted to talk to you about your view of men. I've seen the way you shy away from our male callers, even Isaac. I've found most soldiers to be loyal and kind to their wives. And Ben was—Ben was not a good example for you to look to. I hate to see you waste your life because of that distrust you carry around like a shield. I'm sorry to hear Monroe wasn't kind to you."

Emmie flushed. "It's not that he wasn't kind—" She gulped and sat down. She twisted her hands together in her lap as the other women sat beside her. *It's time for the truth,* she thought. But did she have the strength to tell it? She drew a shaky breath. "I've wanted to tell you about this," she said, slowly searching the faces of her friends. "But I was afraid you wouldn't care for me anymore when you knew the truth."

Amelia leaned forward and took her hand. "Nothing you say could possibly change how we feel about you, Emmie dear. You're our friend, and we love you. Your husband's character can't change yours. You're sweet and loyal and giving. I'm honored to be your friend, and I know Sarah is, too. You can tell us anything, and we won't betray your confidence."

Tears welled up in Emmie's eyes. "I–I don't really know how to begin," she choked.

Sarah handed her a hanky. "Begin wherever you want," she said softly.

"You have to understand. Monroe was so—so alive when I met him. I'd never seen anyone with so much exuberance and energy. I couldn't resist that vitality. When he began to pay attention to me, I couldn't believe it. Me. The slutty daughter of the town drunk."

"Oh, Emmie, you were never that!" Sarah's voice was indignant.

"I heard Mrs. Lambert call me that once when I was thirteen. I've never forgotten it. I'd never even talked to a boy besides my brothers when I heard her say that, but I was so ashamed."

"My mother always talked about how sweet you were and what a shame it was you had to grow up with the father you had," Sarah said.

"Did she really?"

"Really. She would see you at Pap's store. When we'd get home, she'd tell me I should be more like you and not such a tomboy."

A tear slowly slid down Emmie's cheek. "She wouldn't say that now. Not if she knew the truth."

"What truth?" Sarah's voice was insistent.

Emmie took another deep breath. "After Monroe's funeral, a lady showed up at my door. Well-dressed and pretty with a small boy. She was Monroe's true wife, and the little boy was his son. He'd married me although he was already married to her. That's why I had to leave town. So you see," she finished bravely, "the baby I'm carrying is a bastard. And Mrs. Lambert is saying she was right about me all along." The seconds seemed hours as the shock registered on the faces of her friends. Would they reject her, too?

"You poor dear," Amelia said. She jumped to her feet and put her arms around Emmie.

At the compassion in her voice, Emmie burst into tears. Hot, scalding tears that she had kept pent up since she'd first learned the truth about Monroe. There had been no one who could hold her. No one who cared what happened to her.

"It's not your fault, Emmie," Sarah said gently, taking her hand. "You didn't know."

"That's not what they're saying back in Wabash, I'm sure. I was beginning to get some strange looks before I left." Hot blood rushed to her cheeks and she bowed her head.

"But we know you too well to believe any lies," Amelia said. "Why didn't you tell us sooner? Surely you didn't think we wouldn't believe you?"

"I didn't know what to believe. It just hurt too much to talk about or even think about." She got to her feet and hurried to stir the stew before it burned. She turned around and scrubbed the tears from her cheeks with the back of her hand. "I can't tell you how much better it feels now that you know the truth. I've felt badly about deceiving you both. And now you know why I can never trust another man. It hurts too much to find out all their sweet talk is a lie."

Both girls kissed her cheek. "Emmie, dear, God has some-one very special in mind for you," Amelia said. "You'll see. But your secret is safe with us. Now let's have some of that stew."

By the time they ate lunch and cleaned up the kitchen, it was time to go to tea at Frances'. The sun shone weakly in a pale blue sky as they held onto their skirts and hurried across the parade ground. Frances met them at the door with tears in her eyes.

"Why, Frances, dear. Whatever is the matter?" Amelia put an arm around the petite young woman, and Frances promptly burst into sobs.

"I was trying to fix some stew for my husband as a sur-prise. Our cook was late, and I thought I'd try a recipe Mrs. Horton gave me. She said it was foolproof. But she didn't tell me how much of that hateful pressed vegetable cake to put in, so I broke off what I thought was the right amount." She sobbed pitifully and pointed to the kitchen. "Now look. And I wanted it to be so perfect for my first tea party," she wailed.

Globs of stew ran over the big pot and lay deposited like a sticky surprise on the floor. The smell of scorched potatoes and carrots burned their throats with an acrid smoke.

Sarah made a strange, strangling noise, and Emmie looked at her in surprise. *Is she laughing?* She looked closer. Yes, she definitely was, although she was making a valiant attempt to suppress her mirth.

"I'm sorry," Sarah gasped finally, wiping the tears of laughter from her eyes. "I'm just so relieved to find out I'm not the only one who's done something like this. Ask Rand to tell you about my first attempt to cook with those desiccated vegetables."

Frances sobbed one last time, but a glimmer of smile appeared at the corners of her sweetly curving lips. "You did it, too?"

"I did indeed. Only I made a much bigger mess. Don't fret. We'll help you clean it up, and then we'll have tea by the fire."

"I just knew we were going to be good friends!" Frances clapped her hands in delight, then showed them to her rags and water.

"I hear another lady is joining our little band," Mrs. Horton, the doctor's plump and smiling wife, remarked later as she sipped her cup of tea. "Major DuBois is bringing his daughter, Jessica."

"Oh, no!" Sarah and Amelia spoke in unison, and Emmie looked at them with an upraised eyebrow and a question in her violet eyes. Amelia colored and lowered her eyes.

"Jessica DuBois is a bit of a problem," Sarah said hesitantly. "She set her cap for Rand, and she wasn't too pleasant about it. She had the nerve to tell me to go back to Indiana where I belonged. She said I was too starched to know how to deal with a real man. And for a while I was afraid she was right," she added. "I've really tried to get over the way I felt about her, but she makes it hard for any woman to be a real friend to her."

"I'm sure she has her good points," Amelia said. "But Sarah is right—it's hard to find them. But maybe she's changed," she added hopefully.

"You are such an optimist," Sarah said with a loving look at her friend. "You can never seem to admit that some people are just plain rotten through and through. Like—" She broke off with an apologetic look at Emmie.

"Like Ben," Emmie finished for her. "You don't have to mince words on my account, Sarah. When is she coming?" she asked Frances.

"Mrs. Horton says they should arrive any day," Frances said.

"Wonderful," Sarah muttered, taking a bite of her coffee cake. "But it's probably for the best," she said with a shake of her head. "God has been telling me to forgive her, and as long as I didn't have to see her, I've been able to procrastinate. Now I'll have to obey."

"It's going to be a long winter," Amelia sighed.

Two days later they heard that the young lady had indeed arrived. Even if they hadn't been told, they would have known by the way the men acted. They had fewer officers showing up on some pretext to talk with Emmie.

"I'm going to have to swallow my pride and go welcome her to Fort Phil Kearny in a day or two," Sarah groaned. "I'll have to pray for strength."

The next day was colder and more like they had expected late autumn to be. The wind blew ferociously, and the sky was overcast. Emmie offered to take the laundry to Suds Row. Amelia was feeling poorly and let herself be talked into some hot tea with Sarah while Emmie ran across the parade ground to the laundress's cabin. As she passed the sutler's store on the way back, she saw a group of men all clustered around looking in the windows. Curious, she sidled up behind Rooster and tried to see around his scrawny neck.

"Howdy, Miss Emmie." He flushed and backed away from the window a bit.

"What's going on, Rooster?"

"Nothin' much. The men's jest curious about the new gal that come in with the supply train a couple of days ago. She's the daughter of Major DuBois and sure is a looker. Not that it matters to me, of course. She's in there with her pappy and Lieutenant Liddle."

Something squeezed tightly in Emmie's chest. Was Isaac interested in Miss DuBois? She stood on tiptoe and looked in the window. The young woman inside was a real beauty with deep red curls tied back at her long, slim neck. Her dark blue gown enhanced her voluptuous figure and the lace at the neck framed an exquisitely delicate face. She clung to Isaac's arm and gazed up at him adoringly with big blue eyes. Isaac was smiling down at her indulgently. He turned slightly and saw Emmie looking in the window. His eyes widened as they met hers, and he raised a hand involuntarily. Jessica turned to see what he was looking at. She clutched his arm tighter and said something that caused the other men to laugh.

Emmie turned and fled back to the safety of the Campbell quarters. She fought the tears prickling at the back of her throat. Jessica really was a beauty. And an aristocratic one. *With her father's help, a young officer could go far,* she thought. Why was she so upset, anyway? She had made it perfectly clear to Isaac that she wasn't interested.

For the next few days, Emmie threw herself into helping Sarah sew tiny garments for the coming babies. She didn't want to have any time to think. They spent their afternoons with the other women of the fort stitching tiny articles of clothing and learning about child care from the experienced mothers. They worked on Amelia's layette, since her baby was due first. They wanted to make sure everything was ready.

"I wonder where Isaac has been," Amelia remarked on a cold evening as they worked on the final quilt for her little one. "He hasn't been over in several days."

"I noticed that a couple of days ago and asked Rand about

it," Sarah said. "He said he'd invited him several times, but Isaac always had an excuse. He's been acting strange, Rand said. Not his usual cheerful self. And Rand said he thought Jessica had set her cap at him now."

"Not Isaac!" Amelia's voice was alarmed. "We must do something, Sarah."

"What can we do? He has to see through her on his own just like Rand did." Sarah bit off the thread and smoothed the block she was sewing, then sighed. "I know we should stop by and call on her. God has been pressing me about it. I know she needs the Lord, too, but it's so hard to imagine her ever bending her knee to anyone, even God."

Emmie kept her eyes on her needlework, but her heart thumped uncomfortably. Let him shower his attentions on the lovely Jessica! It just goes to show all his pretty words meant nothing, just as she'd known all along. *He is a typical man,* she told herself vehemently.

"Maybe if you invited him over, Emmie," Amelia said thoughtfully. "I thought he seemed to be sweet on you. If you were nice to him, maybe we could get him out of Jessica's clutches."

"Isaac will be fine by himself," Emmie said. "I've told you before I don't intend to get involved with any man."

"But Isaac is different," Sarah said. "He's like Rand and Jake. He has character and principles. And he's a Christian."

"Then he'll see through Jessica on his own." Emmie's tone did not invite further discussion.

"Maybe you're right," Amelia said with a sidelong glance at Sarah. "We'll just have to trust in his good sense. And do a lot of praying," she added.

seven

"Hurry up, Sarah. We're going to be late," Emmie called at the bedroom door. "Assembly sounded five minutes ago, and the post band is warming up."

"I'm coming!" Sarah rushed out in a flurry of rustling skirts and the wafting aroma of lilac. Emmie and Joel followed her out the door and across the parade ground toward the milling crowd in front of headquarters. It was an unseasonably warm day for the last day of October. The sun was so hot, she wished she'd brought her parasol. They hurried up the platform that Colonel Carrington had ordered erected for the ladies and found a seat beside Amelia.

"I thought you were going to miss the opening assembly," Amelia whispered.

Lieutenant Adair, adjutant of the Eighteenth, had the adjutant's call sounded. The companies formed lines in front of their quarters, then moved to their battle positions. Colonel Carrington stepped to the fore and addressed the men. He began a stirring address to dedicate the fort and the brave men who had lost their lives in the course of the fifteen weeks it took to erect the encampment.

Emmie found her eyes straying to Isaac's erect figure just to her left near the newly finished flagpole. He kept his eyes steadfastly on his commanding officer, and she felt a thrill of enjoyment that she could look at him without anyone noticing. He looked very fine with his new blue uniform pressed and the sun glinting off his brass epaulets and polished boots. She glanced to her right and saw Jessica DuBois glaring at her. Her cheeks warm, she looked away quickly and fastened her eyes on Colonel Carrington. The last thing she needed was for Jessica to think she was interested in Isaac!

The little colonel finished his speech by handing the halliards to William Daley, who had done most of the work on the flagpole. The men stood at parade rest with their right hands raised as the orders were barked out. "Attention! Present arms."

The rifles slapped in the hands of the soldiers, and the drum corps played a long roll, followed by the swell of the full band playing "The Star-Spangled Banner." Tears slid down Emmie's cheeks as the guns opened fire, and William Daley pulled the halliards and raised the twenty by thirty-six foot flag slowly to the top of the mast. The warm, gentle breeze stretched it out to its full glory.

She waved her handkerchief in honor of the flag with the rest of the ladies and wept unashamedly. For the first time in her life, she felt part of something worthwhile, something good. She glanced involuntarily over at Isaac and found his steady gaze on her. He smiled and tipped his plumed hat. She smiled tremulously back at him. Glancing over at Jessica, she found the other woman engaged in a conversation with Colonel Carrington. Thank goodness she hadn't seen the exchange!

As the men marched off to their quarters to the tune of "Hail, Columbia," Isaac pushed his way through the melee and caught Emmie's hand.

"Will you save me a dance later? I have to take care of a few duties before I can join the party at headquarters."

"I don't think I'll be dancing. Besides, Jessica might be angry."

He frowned. "What's she got to do with us? Her father is my superior. I've just been helping her get settled in."

"I think she thinks it's more than that." Emmie glanced over and caught Jessica's stare.

Isaac shrugged. "She has nothing to do with us."

"There is no us!"

He sighed. "We'll talk about it later." He strode off in the direction of the barracks.

Emmie bit her lip. *Perhaps I shouldn't go to the party at all,* she thought. She just didn't know how to handle Isaac. Or her own turmoil. For just a moment she longed to be free of the mistrust she felt about men. But it was the only defense she had. And she needed a defense when it came to Isaac.

Amelia grabbed her hand. "Wasn't it wonderful, Emmie? I was so overcome, I cried." She peered in Emmie's face. "You did too, I see!" She tugged her toward the line of ladies and officers heading toward the door to headquarters. "I don't want to miss a moment of the fun. Sarah went to find Rand and Jake. I told her we'd meet them there."

"I'm not sure I should go," Emmie began. "I'm still in mourning—" She broke off at Amelia's incredulous look.

"Don't be ridiculous, Emmie, dear. Whatever do you have to mourn about? That rascal wasn't even your true husband."

"I don't think we've met yet," a soft voice behind them spoke. "Won't you introduce us, Amelia?"

Emmie turned to stare into Jessica's blue eyes. How much did she hear? Emmie's mouth went dry. Did she hear what Amelia said? But the beautiful face before her gave no clue.

"Hello, Jessica," Amelia said. Her voice sounded falsely gay to Emmie, but Jessica didn't seem to notice. "I heard you were here. Sarah and I had planned to stop in yesterday, but she was not feeling well."

"Oh?" The one word and upraised eyebrow spoke volumes. *Sure you were,* it said. *Just as I lost no time in coming to see you.*

Amelia flushed at her tone. "Uhm, this is our dear friend, Emmie Croftner."

"Croftner. Where have I heard that name?" Jessica frowned, a gentle ripple in the smooth perfection of her peaches and cream complexion. "You're not related to Ben?"

"I'm his sister."

"Oh, my." For a moment Jessica seemed flustered. "Do forgive me. I'm very pleased to meet you." She held out a tiny gloved hand, and Emmie clasped it briefly. "Well, I do hope to get to know you better in the future. Now I must go. I see Daddy motioning to me." She gave Emmie an enigmatic look before strolling over to her father.

"I wonder what she's up to," Sarah said as she hurried over to them. "It looked as though she was actually being nice."

"I really don't know," Amelia admitted. "Maybe she's changed, but she seemed quite sweet."

"We can pray," Sarah said with resignation. "God's been telling me to be friends with her, and I know I have to do it, but I haven't been able to gather up enough courage yet."

The furniture had been cleared out of the big meeting room and long tables piled with food lined the west end of the room. The wooden floor had been polished to a brilliant sheen that was a trifle slick to walk on. The band was already warming up at the makeshift bandstand at the other end of the room under the wide eyes of the post children clustered about them. Emmie noticed that Joel had his harmonica with him. She looked around the room and saw Jake wave to them from the food table.

"Trust that man to find the food," Amelia laughed as they threaded their way through the crowd. "Eating already?" she asked with a smile.

"Wait till you taste this apple pie," Jake said, taking an enthusiastic bite. "Mrs. Horton certainly has a way with dried apples."

Amelia pretended to be miffed. "Well, you can just eat at her table every night then. I won't inflict my poor attempt at culinary arts on you."

He put an arm around her. "Now you know I like your cooking just fine."

"Just fine, he says." She punched him gently in the stomach. "When I've been an army wife as long as Mrs. Horton, maybe I'll have a way with dried apples, too."

Emmie gave a wistful chuckle. Sarah and Amelia were so lucky. She pushed the memory of Isaac's smiling eyes away. She would not think about him or any other man!

The band struck up a lively tune behind them, and Jake took Amelia into his arms. "Time's a-wasting, gal." Amelia laughed as he swung her onto the dance floor.

Rand claimed Sarah a few moments later, and the officers began to line up for a dance with Emmie. She was exhausted within fifteen minutes. The men were so exuberant and determined to have a good time. When there was no lady available, they danced with one another. She passed from one set of arms to another until the faces all became a blur.

"I think this is my dance." Isaac cut in on a young lieutenant with a good-natured grin. He spun Emmie away from the disappointed young man. "You look very lovely tonight."

Emmie looked away, a tide of red rising in her cheeks. Why did he always have to embarrass her? "It was a very nice ceremony," she said awkwardly.

"Wasn't it?" He drew her closer as the music changed to a slower song and laid his chin on the top of her head. "You are just the right height," he said softly.

Emmie felt herself relaxing against his chest. She heard the thud of his heart under her ear and smelled the pine scent of his soap. *If I could just stay like this forever,* she thought dreamily before she caught herself. No! She pulled away slightly. That was how Monroe had trapped her before. Him with his sweet talk and tender arms. She was soiled goods now, too. Isaac wouldn't be interested in her if he knew the truth.

"Isaac, I've been looking for you everywhere," a honeyed voice said. "Daddy wants to talk to you." Jessica laid a gloved hand on Isaac's arm and gazed up at him with an adorable pout on her lips.

"I'll be along in a moment," he said, pulling away from her gently. "Let me get Emmie some punch first."

"No, really, I'm fine," Emmie stammered. She stepped away from him hastily. "You go on along with Jessica. I've promised the next dance to Jake."

Isaac hesitated, then allowed Jessica to pull him away.

Emmie looked after them with a faint film of tears in her eyes. *Why on earth am I crying,* she wondered. Isaac meant nothing to her and never could. She blinked the tears away just before Jake came to claim her for his dance.

"Amelia is determined not to let me sit by her all evening. She says she likes watching us dance as much as if she could dance every dance herself," Jake said as they swung into a rollicking galop.

Emmie was breathless by the time they finished the dance. Jake took her elbow and guided her toward the punch table. "I wanted a chance to tell you how much I appreciated the help you've been to Amelia," he said as he handed her a glass of punch. "She was so lonely and blue before you and Sarah came. I haven't caught her crying once since the two of you arrived."

"I haven't done anything," Emmie said with a blush. "Sarah is the real miracle worker." She looked away and took a sip of punch. Sarah had told her it was just strong tea with citric acid in it, but it was really quite good.

"That's not true, you know," he said with a frown. "I've seen the way you hover in the background trying to make sure neither one are doing too much. You have a sweet, unassuming way of encouragement about you that has really helped Amelia."

Emmie's blush deepened. "I'm glad if I've been able to help her," she stammered. "There's no one in the world like Amelia. She's so trusting of everyone and sees the best in everyone she meets. I wish I could be more like her."

Jake smiled. "She's too trusting sometimes. But you're right—there's no one like her."

"You love her very much."

He nodded. "She means everything in the world to me. I don't know what I'd do if anything ever happened to her." He looked over to where Amelia sat chatting with Mrs. Horton. "She seems so frail, sometimes it worries me."

Emmie laid a hand on his arm. "She'll be just fine. Dr.

Horton is very pleased with her condition. Women have babies all the time, you know."

Jake squeezed her hand. "You're right, I'm sure. Anyway, thank you for all your help."

"You're very welcome." She watched him stride over to his wife, whose face lit up as she saw him coming. Emmie couldn't suppress the pang of envy that pierced her heart. Love like that would never be for her. She sighed and took the last sip of her punch before being claimed for another dance.

※

The next morning dawned bright and clear. Emmie slipped out of bed and poured cold water from the cracked pitcher into the bowl on the cloth-covered crate that passed as a bed stand. She shivered as she took a piece of flannel and quickly washed herself in the frigid water. She pulled on her blue wool dress and combed her hair up into a serviceable knot, then draped her shawl around her shoulders. She could hear Rand thumping around in the kitchen as he readied for his day. The clear notes of reveille sounded just as she pushed open the curtain from her bedroom and stepped into the small parlor.

Rand looked up as she entered. "Go on back to sleep. I wouldn't let Sarah get up, either. I'll grab some grub at mess so you girls don't have to worry about fixing me breakfast."

"I don't mind," she protested.

He patted her shoulder as he strode by and seized his coat. "I know you don't, but I have a busy day today, and I might as well get to it. You get some rest." He opened the door and stepped out into the still dark morning. "I'll see you tonight," he said before closing the door.

Now what was she supposed to do? She was already dressed and too wide awake to go back to sleep. She tiptoed past Joel, a lump under the covers on the parlor cot with just a tuft of red hair showing, to the bedroom door and peered in at Sarah.

"Rand wouldn't let me get up," Sarah murmured sleepily

when she saw her at the door. "I really should, though. I need to take the laundry to Suds Row."

"I'll do it. I'm already dressed and not a bit sleepy. Would you like some breakfast before I go?"

"No thanks." Sarah yawned and pulled the quilts up higher on her shoulders. "All I want to do is sleep."

"That's fine. You get some rest. I'll stop over and check on Amelia after I drop off the laundry." Emmie closed the door gently. She was so glad her own morning sickness had lasted such a short time and she felt well enough to continue to be a help to Sarah. She threw some more wood in the fire, put a pot of coffee on to boil, and cut a slice of bread for breakfast. By the time she slathered jam on it and gulped it and two cups of coffee down, the bugle sounded fatigue call. She gathered up the laundry into a basket and stepped outside, as men from various parts of the fort hurried to fall in and find out what their duties would be for the morning.

The sun was just beginning to send pink streaks across the eastern sky as she skirted the parade ground and hurried toward Suds Row. Every fort had a Soapsuds Row, or Suds Row as it was more commonly called. The laundresses were usually either the wives of enlisted men or immigrant women with red, chapped hands and well-developed muscles in their arms and shoulders. Emmie stopped at the first tent she came to. A kettle of water belched out lye-scented steam, but the laundress was nowhere in sight. She set her burden down and rubbed her back, a bit sore from the evening's festivities.

As she looked around, she saw a pair of blue eyes regarding her seriously from behind the flap of the tent.

"Hello, what's your name?"

The child didn't answer but cautiously stepped out from the protecting flap of the tent. A small girl about two years old with a tangled mass of nearly black curls, big blue eyes, and chubby dimpled cheeks gazed up at her.

"Aren't you adorable!" Emmie exclaimed. "Won't you tell me your name?"

The little girl popped a thumb in her mouth, then took it out long enough to say, "Mary," before sticking it back in her mouth.

"Well, Mary, do you know where I might find your mama?" Emmie knelt in front of the tiny girl and touched the dark curls.

At that moment a young woman scurried from behind the tent with an armload of uniforms. "Sorry I am if ye had to wait, missy," she gasped in a broad Irish lilt. "I didn't know ye were here." Her face softened as she saw Emmie kneeling before the little girl. "I be seeing you've made the acquaintance of me sister."

Sister? Emmie had assumed the child was the woman's daughter. They both possessed the same dark curls and deep blue eyes. But as she looked closer, she realized the young woman was hardly more than a child herself. Certainly no more than fifteen or sixteen. "Are you the laundress or should I talk to your mother?" she asked hesitantly.

The young woman dropped the uniforms beside the kettle of water. "Sure and it's myself, Maggie O'Donnell, you'll be wanting, miss. Me mam, God rest her soul, has been with the angels these last two years. The childbed fever took her when Mary here was only six days old."

"I'm sorry." Emmie was intrigued with the energetic young woman. A child raising a child. From her accent, she wasn't too long out of the potato fields of Ireland. "How long have you been in America?"

Maggie dumped a uniform into a galvanized tub and proceeded to scrub it vigorously against the washboard. "Me da brought us to the wondrous city of New York just four months before Mary arrived. He took a job with the railroad and moved us to Chicago. But the Lord saw fit to take him of the consumption before he clapped eyes on Mary." She leaned forward and said in a whisper, "Between you and mé, miss, I think me mum died of a broken heart. She had no reason to go on with me da gone."

"And you've been all alone since?"

"Just me and Mary taking care of each other."

"How did you get out here in the wilderness?" Emmie was fascinated by the young woman's self-confidence and independence.

"A chum of me da's heard the army had a need for a washerwoman out here and arranged for me to have the job. It's hard work, it is, but honest." She saw the expression on Emmie's face. "But don't feel sorry for me, miss. It's better work than I could get in Chicago. The only offer I had there was in a bawdry house. But I'd have taken even that if it meant the difference between watching young Mary starve or no." Maggie stood and pushed a stray black curl out of her eyes. "When you be needing your laundry done by?"

"Tomorrow is soon enough," Emmie said. The last thing she wanted to do was add to this young woman's burden.

"Won't be no problem at all. It's been real nice talking to you. Most ladies don't bother with the likes of me." Maggie grinned cheerfully. "Not that I'm complaining, mind you. I don't have nothing in common with those high-falutin' types anyhow. But you're different, miss."

"Please call me Emmie." She held out her hand.

Maggie eyed her outstretched hand cautiously before wiping her own water-roughened hand against her apron and taking Emmie's fingers gingerly. "Pleased to meet you, Miss Emmie."

"Just Emmie. I'd like to be friends." She didn't know why it was so important to her, but it was. There was something about the young woman that drew her irresistibly. She didn't know if it was Maggie's indomitable spirit or harsh circumstances, but she just knew that she wanted to be able to call her a friend.

Maggie's eyes grew wide. "Friends with the likes of me," she said incredulously. Unexpectedly her eyes welled with tears. "Don't mind me," she sniffled. "Ever since we got here, it's like I'm a spirit or something. The other ladies all look through me, and I can tell they think Mary is me own lovely daughter and that I'm an indecent woman."

Emmie's throat grew thick with her own tears. What would everyone think of her if they knew the truth? "I'll be back tomorrow," she promised. Emmie waved to little Mary and set off toward Amelia's quarters. She was awed by Maggie's spirit and courage. At least Emmie had Sarah and Rand to look to for support. The young washerwoman had no one, but was still able to smile at circumstances and find a way to support herself and her sister with honest hard work. Emmie wondered if she was a Christian, too, like the Campbells. Maggie's courage shamed her.

Amelia had insisted that she just let herself in whenever she wanted to stop by, so Emmie just rapped once on the door and slipped inside. Amelia looked up with a forced smile from her seat on the cot that served as a sofa in the parlor.

"I was hoping you'd stop by," she said. "I was just sitting here feeling sorry for myself." Her smile was gone and tears hung on her dark lashes.

"Why whatever is wrong?" Emmie quickly crossed the room to put her arms around her.

"I'm just being a silly goose," Amelia sniffed. "For the first time I'm really frightened about having this baby. What if something's wrong with it? Or I could die and leave Jake all alone with a child to raise. Women do die in childbirth, you know."

Emmie hugged her. "You'll be fine, I know. You're strong and healthy," she said with more conviction than she felt. She and Sarah had discussed how fragile their friend had been looking the last few weeks.

"I'm not afraid to die, you know. I know I'll be with the Lord, but I just don't want to leave Jake all alone." Amelia scrubbed at her cheeks with the back of her hand, then turned and looked Emmie squarely in the face. "There is one thing you could do that would make me feel better."

"Anything. You want a cup of tea?" Emmie half rose to her feet, but Amelia pulled her back down and gripped her arms.

"I want you to promise that if anything happens to me,

you'll marry Jake and take care of him and the baby."

Emmie caught her breath. What was Amelia saying? She tried to draw away, but Amelia kept a tight grip on her arms.

"I mean it, Emmie. I've thought about it a lot. It would solve your problems, too. Jake would love your baby. He loves children, you know. It would make me feel so much better if I was sure they would be all right no matter what happens."

Emmie couldn't think with Amelia's beseeching blue eyes fastened on her. How could she ask such a thing? But Amelia had never been like other women. She always thought of others first and never seemed to consider her own feelings. "You can't just plan Jake's life for him like that," she said desperately.

"Jake has already agreed," Amelia said with a brave smile. "He pooh-poohed my fears, but he said he'd do whatever I wanted if the worst happened."

For an instant a vague image of red hair and blue eyes swam across Emmie's vision, but she pushed it away. That wasn't reality. Her friend was reality. But really, what were the odds of anything happening to Amelia? She was just suffering from pregnancy jitters. Everything would be fine; she just needed a little assurance right now. "I promise," she said reluctantly.

Amelia smiled with relief. "I feel so much better. Now I'll take that cup of tea."

As Emmie put the kettle on the stove and threw more wood in the fire, she fought down a sense of panic at the thought of her promise. What about her promise to herself never to trust another man enough to marry? But this was different, she told herself. Amelia's God would not allow anything bad to happen to her. And besides, Jake was totally trustworthy. She just couldn't see herself married to him. But she wouldn't have to worry about that, she told herself as she brought the cup of tea to Amelia. She would watch over her friend better than her own mother would. Another month and the baby would be born. Amelia would put these silly fears to rest.

eight

By the next day both Amelia and Sarah had recovered their health and high spirits. Emmie couldn't wait to tell them about Maggie.

"I think it's lovely for you to befriend her," Amelia said after Emmie's explanation. "And we will certainly have her to tea. But you should know that the other women will disapprove. Army life is so regulated, and fraternizing with the enlisted men is frowned on here."

"But she's not an enlisted man," Emmie protested. "She's just a lonely young woman with no friends. I don't see how being a friend to her could hurt."

"I know it's hard to understand," Sarah said. "But there's a very rigid code of behavior in the army, and the laundresses are considered beyond polite society by most gentlewomen."

Emmie stared at them in bewilderment. "The one thing I've always noticed about army people is how friendly they are and how easily they welcome new people to the post. Why would they feel that way about someone who earns her living by her own hard work?"

"It's not that they don't believe in hard work," Amelia explained. "It really goes back to when laundresses were kept women who followed after the troops to see to the needs of their men. In the past many were, well I don't like to say it, but they were scarlet women. Nowadays, many are wives of enlisted men, too. Fraternizing with an enlisted man's wife is just the same as being friends with him."

So what does that say about me? Emmie wondered. *Does that mean the people who act so kind and friendly now would shun me if they knew the truth?*

Sarah saw the stricken look on Emmie's face. "I'm sorry if

we upset you, Emmie. We just wanted you to know what the situation is like here. Of course, we don't feel that way and we would love to meet young Maggie."

"It's not that," Emmie said, her face flushing with suppressed tears. "I know you'll both like her as much as I did. It's just that my reputation would be much worse than hers if the people just knew about Monroe. Maybe I should leave. If your other friends would frown on associating with Maggie, they would really be disgusted with me. The truth will probably come out sooner or later. It always does."

"Oh, Emmie, anyone who knows you at all knows you're much too trusting and innocent. They would know you were just deceived by a scoundrel. No one would blame you." Amelia put her arms around her. "You put any thought of leaving us right out of your head. Besides, it's much too dangerous right now to even think about leaving the fort."

Emmie was unconvinced, although she let her friends lead her to the kitchen for a cup of tea and some bread with jam. The shame she'd pushed to the back of her mind swelled up again. No amount of love and acceptance would erase it. Maybe she should just confess it to the world instead of trying to pretend to be something she wasn't. She was sure Jessica wouldn't be as charitable about her innocence as Amelia and Sarah were.

That night as she crawled under her quilts and breathed in the scent of her hay-filled mattress, she tried to think about what she could do if she left here. She was still awake at the two o'clock sentry call. As she heard the familiar "All's well," tears leaked out of the corners of her eyes. All was not well for her. There was nothing else she could do but trust in the mercy of her friends for now. Maybe when spring came, she could think of some way to support herself and the baby. She felt so empty inside. How did her friends remain so calm and assured? Perhaps it was their faith in God. She shivered a little at the sudden thought. Could that be the reason? But God seemed very far away from her, beyond her reach. She was certainly undeserving of any attention from Him.

The next morning Emmie was heavy-eyed and lethargic. She knew her friends worried about her, but no one could help her with her private battle. The week sped by and she was eager to attend the Sunday service. She'd thought often about what the minister had said about God caring for her. She didn't see how He could. Not after all the things she'd done.

This week he began by reading Isaiah 1:18. " 'Come now, and let us reason together, saith the Lord: though your sins be as scarlet, they shall be as white as snow; though they be red like crimson, they shall be as wool.' " The young minister cleared his throat and his eyes seemed to look right into Emmie's. "No matter what you've done with your life, God can forgive it—He wants to forgive it. But you have to be ready to acknowledge your sin to Him. God is the only one you can truly tell your innermost thoughts, doubts, and fears. We all wrestle with our private doubts and troubles, but God can bring the peace and contentment you're longing for. Running away from a situation won't bring peace. Only Christ can do that."

He continued on with the sermon, but Emmie didn't hear anything else he said. Her throat burned with unshed tears as she considered his words. Peace and contentment. Was there such a thing for her? The very words seemed alien, meant for someone else. The home she'd grown up in was anything but peaceful. Her father was always shouting and cursing, her brothers, especially Ben, filled with even more anger than her father. As the minister reached the end of his sermon, he asked the congregation to bow their heads. Emmie closed her eyes and felt her heart opening like a sponge, ready for the living water the preacher had spoken about. *Lord, if You'll have me, I want to give my life to You.* Tears slid silently down her cheeks. *Forgive my sins and make me as wool. You know how scarlet my sins are. Wash them away and bring me peace.*

As the preacher ended his closing prayer and the congregation rose, Emmie felt as though she was about to float off the floor. She felt new and clean. Was this what peace was?

After the service, she told her friends what she'd done, and they cried and rejoiced with her. She felt as though she could face anything with the Lord beside her. She'd always been so fearful. Of what, she didn't really know, but the terror had always been there. Ready to spring upon her like a cougar on an unwary doe. Now she felt strong and capable. Even the thought of the life stirring within her didn't fill her with gut-wrenching fear anymore. For the first time in her life, Emmie felt as though she mattered. She mattered enough for Jesus to die for her. That fact changed everything.

She and her friends spent most afternoons the next few weeks curled up by the fire in the parlor reading the Bible and discussing different passages. There was so much to learn, so much she'd never heard about. As soon as she read Philippians 4:13, she knew it had been written just for her. "I can do all things through Christ which strengtheneth me." The verse was a litany that sounded in her head all the time. Every time a twinge of doubt in herself would raise its ugly head, the comforting words would subdue all her fears.

Isaac stopped by every couple of nights, but she had no opportunity to talk with him alone. Not that she wanted to, of course. He rejoiced with them at the news of her salvation.

Emmie was so full of contagious joy and courage that Sarah was emboldened to go across the parade ground to the DuBois residence. Jessica had ushered her in, but she laughed when she'd asked her forgiveness, Sarah told Emmie later. Jessica told her she didn't want anything to do with God or Sarah's self-righteous pap and showed her the door. Sarah just seemed to pray for her more often. She told Emmie she thought she saw tears in Jessica's eyes for a moment.

❧

As November began, winter settled its icy claws more firmly into the little fort community. Cold, piercing winds, mountains of snowdrifts, and bitter cold kept the ladies constantly looking for ways to keep warm. The wood details, escorted by guards, went out every day but could barely keep up with the demand, even though wood had been stockpiled for several months. The ladies ventured out only when absolutely necessary. Even a brisk walk from quarters to quarters left them numb with cold.

Emmie couldn't remember a time when she didn't ache with cold. The wind howled around the tiny fort like a pack of ravenous wild dogs, poking icy fangs through her skirts that chilled her to the bone. Early one cold morning, she bundled her cloak around her as tightly as she could before picking up her basket and heading for the sutler's store. Sarah had been craving fruit, any fruit, so Emmie thought she would see what was available. The price would be dear, but Rand had told her to get whatever she could find. He worried a lot about his wife these days. Sarah seemed pale and listless, but Emmie thought it was the confinement of the tiny fort and the especially cold weather they'd been enduring that caused her friend's wan appearance. There had been constant skirmishes with the Indians, and the little graveyard beside the fort received a newly fallen soldier almost every day. The ever-present fear hung like black crepe over the encampment.

She staggered to keep her balance in the wind as she hurried as fast as she could toward the sutler's store. As she passed the DuBois residence, she saw Jessica motion to her. What now? She stopped for a moment before obeying her imperious summons. She had managed to avoid any contact with Jessica since the dance and since Sarah's encounter with her. The cold air followed her into the foyer as Jessica shut the door behind them. Emmie glanced around quickly as she followed Jessica into the parlor. The fireplace blazed with warmth and cast a golden glow over the gleaming mahogany furniture. The parlor looked lovely and welcoming, but the look on Jessica's face was just the opposite.

"I've been watching for you," Jessica said. "You haven't

been out much." Her eyes swept contemptuously over Emmie's plain gray dress and bonnet.

"Sarah hasn't been well. I really can't stay. I need to get back to her as quickly as possible," Emmie said timidly. She shrank away from the cold smile on Jessica's face. She couldn't imagine what Jessica would want with her. And what did that triumphant glint in her eye mean? Her nervousness increased a notch as Jessica allowed a strained pause to drag out.

"This won't take long," she said finally with another chilly smile. "I just thought it was important that we get a few things settled between us."

"What kinds of things?" Emmie's agitation grew as Jessica stepped in closer. Her sweet, overpowering scent made Emmie's head swim.

"I've seen the way you look at Isaac. My father wants me to marry him, and I intend to do just that. Rand chose that chit of a girl over me, and I refuse to be humiliated again." She pushed her face into Emmie's. "I know all about you, Miss Croftner. I contacted a cousin who made some inquiries for me. I know that the child you're carrying is a bastard and you've never been married. If you force me to, I'll let everyone here know all about it."

Emmie felt faint. This was her nightmare come true. She couldn't stand for anyone to know about her shame. It would reflect on her friends, too. She clutched icy hands in the folds of her cloak and swallowed hard.

Jessica saw her white face and smiled again. "You are to stay away from Isaac. Make it clear you have no interest in him at all. If you don't, I'll have no choice but to let everyone know you lived with a man out of wedlock."

"But I thought I was married!" Emmie protested. "It wasn't like you're making it sound."

"Look at you! Why would anyone marry you except for your money? If you were too stupid to figure out what the man was after, that's your problem." She flicked a disparaging hand at Emmie. "Oh, you're not unattractive, I suppose. That helpless look probably brings out the protective nature in some men. But the apple doesn't fall far from the tree, you know. You're no better than your brothers, and anyone who knows them would instantly know what kind of person you are behind that little-girl-lost facade."

Emmie paled and tears pooled in the corners of her eyes. She willed them not to fall with a fierce determination. She didn't want to let Jessica see how much her words had hurt her. Monroe had told her she was beautiful, but she'd always known it couldn't be true. She'd been so foolish. So easily swayed by Monroe's smooth words. She swallowed hard and stiffened her shoulders. "You needn't worry about me, Miss DuBois. I have no interest in Isaac. He is merely a friend."

Jessica's eyes narrowed as she stared at Emmie. "I certainly hope that's true. For your sake, it had better be." She opened the door and practically pushed Emmie through it. "And don't tell anyone about our conversation. Not if you want your little secret to remain between the two of us."

Emmie found herself staring at the brass knocker as the door slammed behind her. She gulped and forced herself to walk down the steps on shaky legs. She had always hated confrontation of any kind. It brought back too many bad memories of the constant barrage of abuse her father had heaped on her head. No matter what went wrong when she was growing up, it was always her fault. If Ben spilled his glass of milk, it was because Emmie filled it too full. If Labe forgot to feed the stock when it was his turn, it was because Emmie forgot to remind him. She swallowed the lump in her throat. No one must know. She couldn't bear it if Sarah and Amelia were hurt because of her foolishness over Monroe.

The walk in the cold wind stiffened her resolve, and she had quit shaking by the time she pushed open the door to the sutler's store. The smell struck her as she stepped across the threshold. The overpowering stench of unwashed bodies mixed with cinnamon, coffee, tobacco, and vinegar from the pickle keg nearly gagged her. She quickly picked up a handful of wrinkled apples and paid for them, aware of the stares of the Indians and soldiers alike. The sutler's store was always such a trial to endure. It wasn't so bad when she was escorted by Rand or Jake, but a young woman alone attracted a lot of attention.

She escaped into the fresh air and hurried back to the Campbell quarters. Sarah looked up as she burst through the door. Emmie had intended to tell her friend about the confrontation with Jessica, but after one look at Sarah's pale, pinched face, she decided against it. Now was the perfect time to put into practice what she'd been learning the past few weeks. She whispered a silent prayer and turned the whole matter over to God. He would take care of it. He'd promised to take care of her and He would. She put on a bright smile as she closed the door behind her.

"I found some lovely apples at the sutler's store," she said proudly. "They're a little wrinkly, but they don't seem to have any bad spots. Here, smell." She put a small apple under Sarah's nose. "They should make delicious apple dumplings."

Sarah took the apple slowly and sniffed. A ghost of a smile brightened her face, then she lay back against the cushions on the parlor cot. "You are a dear." She handed the apple back to Emmie. "I don't know why I feel so poorly," she sighed. "The winter is just beginning and already the wind is about to drive me mad."

Emmie sat beside her and put an arm around her slim shoulders. "God is here with you, though. I have so much peace since I realized that. Now the vastness that used to terrify me when I looked around outside just reminds me how powerful He is."

Sarah smiled at her. "You put me to shame sometimes, Emmie. You're right, of course. I shouldn't complain. At least I'm here with Rand and not stuck back east with my brother. God has been good to us. With all the fighting going on, Rand hasn't been wounded and neither has Jake. We should count our blessings."

Emmie hugged her again. "I think I'll get started on those apple dumplings. You rest a while." She stood and went to the kitchen, all of three steps away. She hummed as she took down her apron and wrapped it around her waist. Hmm, it seemed her waist had thickened just since yesterday. She took down a tin of flour and dumped some into a bowl. "What time did Rand say to expect him?" she asked.

"He sent Joel by to tell us he'd be late. That reckless Lieutenant Fetterman has finally talked Colonel Carrington into letting him try an ambush. The colonel asked Rand to go along to keep Fetterman out of trouble. They're taking some mules as bait, but Joel said Rand thought it was a harebrained scheme. Red Cloud is no fool, but Fetterman is hotheaded and thinks all Indians are stupid and slow."

Emmie sighed. Always there was fighting. Every day, every hour they listened for the crack of rifles in the cold winter air and the war whoops of the Sioux. There was never a respite. As she kneaded the dough and sliced the apples, she and Sarah chatted about everything except the one thing they both listened for. Through the long afternoon and early evening, they waited and talked to fill the waiting. Only when they heard Rand's boot heels and Joel's excited chatter as they came up the front porch did they relax.

Rand came in, stomping his feet in the entry and reminding Joel to do the same. His face was pale and pinched with the cold. Sarah rushed to help him out of his snow-covered greatcoat. He shrugged it off and dropped onto the cot with a sigh. He held out his hands toward the roaring fire as Sarah sat beside him.

"I expected you before now," she said softly.

"You should have seen it," Joel put in excitedly. "I was watching from the blockhouse. The Sioux knew it was a trap. They just waited Fetterman out, then slipped behind the fort and stampeded the cattle. Fetterman looked as savage as a meat axe."

"Joel!" Sarah spoke sharply.

He looked sheepish. "Well, that's what Rooster said."

"You're not to talk disrespectful of your elders."

Her brother scuffed a toe on the floor. "He sure was mad, though. He told the colonel he wanted to go out after them right then and there, but the colonel wouldn't let him. He stomped off with Lieutenant Grummond. They were both grumbling."

Emmie broke in hurriedly. "Your supper's ready." She didn't want to hear about any more battles. She watched as Sarah put a hand on Rand's arm, then hurried to fix him a plate of thick stew and warm slices of bread with butter. She fixed a smaller plate for Joel.

"Joel's right," Rand said after a few bites of supper. "Fetterman is spoiling for a fight with the Sioux. He's going to wind up with his hair lifted if he isn't careful. He's rash, and I'm afraid he'll drag Lieutenant Grummond into a losing battle with him. Neither one of them have any respect for the way an Indian can fight. They haven't been out here long enough to have a little sense knocked into them."

Emmie shuddered. She'd seen Lieutenant Fetterman around. He usually had a group of starry-eyed soldiers around listening to stories of his exploits in the War Between the States. His bragging and posturing repelled her and filled her with a strange foreboding. The tiny quarters seemed even more claustrophobic than usual. She desperately wished for a walk outside, but she could hear the wind howling around the windows. She jumped as someone pounded on the door, then hurried to open it.

Isaac's broad shoulders filled the doorway. The snow swirled around him like a thick, wet fog. "Come in," she gasped as the freezing wind took her breath away.

He pushed past her and she shut the door. "We've got a visitor," he said to Sarah. "I told her to come in with me, but she insisted I come and ask if it's all right."

Sarah looked up at him anxiously. "Is Amelia all right?"

Isaac grinned. "It's got nothing to do with her. This is a

visitor the Lord has blown our way. I think you'll be right happy to see her."

Sarah gave him a fierce look and he laughed. "I think it should be a surprise in spite of what she says." He turned and opened the door again. "Come on in," he said gently.

A figure covered in a thick buffalo hide slowly stepped through the doorway. Emmie was startled to realize it was an Indian girl of about sixteen or seventeen. Her thick braids were coated with snow and she looked pale and emaciated.

The young woman stared straight at Sarah, then smiled. "My Say-rah, do you not know me?"

Sarah gasped and jumped to her feet. "Morning Song!" She literally ran toward the young woman with her arms out-stretched. "I didn't know if I'd ever see you again." She put her arms around the young woman and burst into tears.

Tears leaked from Morning Song's eyes as she shrugged off the buffalo robe and revealed a baby snuggled against her breast in an Indian carrier of some sort. The child, a boy, slept peacefully with his thumb corked in his mouth.

"Oh, Morning Song, you have a baby!" Sarah held out her hands. "May I?"

The Indian girl nodded and gently lifted her child out of the carrier and put him into Sarah's outstretched arms. Sarah cradled him and crooned to him softly.

Emmie noticed the child had light hair. *His father must be white,* she thought. She wondered who the young woman was. Sarah was obviously very fond of her. She'd heard Sarah talk about the time she'd spent in an Indian camp and her friends there, but the only Indian woman she'd heard her mention was one called White Beaver. Who was this girl? She had once been beautiful, Emmie was sure. Now her hair was dull and lifeless from hunger and deprivation and the sparkle was gone from her large dark eyes.

The men stood around smiling foolishly. Rand seemed glad to see Morning Song as well. Joel was immediately pestering her about news of someone called Red Hawk. Emmie stood a little apart, feeling slightly left out. She had no idea who Morning Song was or why they were all so glad to see her. Isaac saw her confused look and stepped nearer.

"She was one of Sarah's first students back at Fort Laramie when Sarah taught reading and writing to the Indian youngsters," Isaac explained softly. A dawning look broke over his face and he colored. "Um, your brother, Ben, was, uh, married. Well, not really married." He broke off in embarrassment, then plunged ahead. "Anyway, Emmie, that baby is your nephew. Ben had mistreated her and Sarah got her away from him. She disappeared shortly after that and we haven't seen her since. She came in a little while ago with some friendly Shoshone."

The words didn't make sense. Her nephew. Emmie looked across the room at the sleeping child. Her feet drew her across the floor until she stood in front of Sarah. She gazed down into the face of the baby boy. Ben's son? He did have a certain look of her brother. His eyes were the same smoky gray. His hair was darker than Ben's but not the raven of Morning Song's.

Sarah was suddenly aware of her standing there. The same dawning comprehension filled her face as had been on Isaac's. She could tell by looking at Emmie that she knew who the baby was. After a glance at her Indian friend, she gently placed the child into Emmie's arms. "What is his name, Morning Song?" Sarah asked.

"I call him John. I learn about John in Holy Book when I go to mission school. About how he teach others to love God. So I name him John Randall. My people, my father, call him White Buffalo."

Rand jerked his head up, then a delighted grin stole over his face. "You named him after me?"

Morning Song nodded slowly. "You and Say-rah my friends. I want for John to be fine man like you. Not like—" She broke off and took a deep breath.

Not like Ben, Emmie finished for her silently. She approached the young woman warily. Would she hate her when she knew she was sister to the man who'd used her? "I am your sister," she said gently. "Ben was my brother."

Morning Song flinched back as though Emmie had struck her. "You have her here?" she cried to Sarah. "Sister of my enemy?"

She whirled as though to flee before she remembered Emmie still held her child. She snatched her son from Emmie's arms, then realized Emmie was crying. She searched Emmie's eyes, probing secrets from her soul. The tension eased out of her shoulders, and she gently handed young John back to Emmie.

"You my sister. Ben hurt you, too."

How did she know that? Emmie accepted the child again with wonder. What had Morning Song seen in her eyes? The baby had awakened from all the fuss and played with strands of her hair that had escaped its confinement. She hugged him gently, then gave him back to Morning Song. "You have a beautiful son," she said softly.

Morning Song smiled and spoke softly to the baby as she eased him back into the carrier. "Ben is here?" she asked.

Sarah saw the fear and tension on her face and hurried to reassure her. "Oh, no, Morning Song. He's—" She broke off and bit her lip as she glanced at Emmie.

Emmie took a deep breath and finished Sarah's sentence for her. "He's dead. Killed by Sioux." At least they thought that was true. And even if he wasn't, Morning Song would never have to worry about him again.

"When this happen?" Morning Song looked puzzled.

"Shortly after you left Fort Laramie. He was killed in a fall from a horse, Labe said."

Morning Song shook her head. "Then it not Ben. My brother see him at Sioux hunting grounds. Near the mountain where the white men take the yellow rock not many moons ago."

"You mean the gold mines in Montana?" Rand asked incredulously.

Morning Song nodded. "My brother want to kill him, but too many white men around with guns."

The only sound was the crackle from the fire as everyone digested the news. Ben was alive! *But he'd left Labe behind,* Emmie thought. Why would he do that?

"I can't believe it," Rand said finally. "All this time we were sure he was dead. Do you know if Labe found him in the goldfields?"

Morning Song shrugged. "I not know. Red Hawk only see Ben."

Sarah put her arm around Morning Song. "There's so much to tell you. Come over by the fire and rest. You'll stay here with us, of course."

Morning Song wilted visibly and she began to tremble. "It is more than I hoped for, my Say-rah. I just wished to see you again. I go back to the camp."

"You'll do no such thing," Rand put in firmly. "You need to rest and get your strength back. We can make up a bed for you in the kitchen near the stove."

"She can have my place here in the parlor," Joel said eagerly. "I can stay with Jake and Amelia."

"Good idea," Rand said. "Is Red Hawk with you, Morning Song? He can stay with Joel."

The young woman bowed her head in sorrow. "He and my father are with Red Cloud."

The announcement left them all speechless for a moment, then Rand said gently, "We'll pray for him that God will keep him safe."

Isaac left, and the others spent the rest of the evening curled around the fire talking. Baby John was passed from arm to arm and slept contentedly through it. Morning Song told them she had gone with her father to the winter hunting grounds after leaving Fort Laramie. She had wanted to kill herself when she discovered she was to have a baby. But the truths she'd learned at the missionary school had kept her from such a drastic step. She knew Jesus loved her and would take care of her and her baby somehow. The Sioux did not treat her well as her pregnancy started to show. After John was born, she could no longer tolerate the unkind remarks about him, so she slipped away with the Shoshone chief who stopped in their village to speak with her father. She knew if she could get to one of the bluecoat forts, she could find where Sarah and Rand were. Jesus had led her right to them, she told them.

Rand stoked the fire for the night and yawned. "I'm ready for some shut-eye. You better head on over to Jacob's, Joel. Take some blankets with you so you don't have to wake them." Sarah was drooping with weariness as he led her off to bed. After Joel hurried out with an armload of blankets, Emmie made up the bed for Morning Song, then slipped away to her own bed. As she snuggled under the buffalo robe, she thought about how God had taken care of the young Indian woman. A sense of God's arms around her brought a smile to her face. He truly did care, didn't He? She could rest upon His promises. He would care for her just as He did Morning Song.

nine

The dawn brought a blizzard with it as snow joined the howling wind of the night before. The swirling snow blotted out the sun and blew through the cracks in the house. Emmie shivered as she lit her lamp and quickly washed with her flannel and dressed in the blue wool. As she pulled her curtain back, she could hear Morning Song crooning to baby John. She was eager to see both Morning Song and the baby again.

Morning Song looked up from her seat by the kitchen stove as Emmie hurried toward her. "You up early," she said. "Say-rah still sleeping."

"Has Rand left?" Emmie asked as she poured hot water into the teapot.

Morning Song nodded as she went to lay the baby down in the parlor. She covered him with the edge of the buffalo robe and came back into the kitchen. "Baby up most of the night. Not used to house."

Emmie tried to imagine living out on the plains in a tepee and shivered. She poured herself and Morning Song a cup of tea.

Morning Song smiled as she spooned sugar into her tea and picked up her cup gently. "Many moons since I have tea with Say-rah." She sighed and took a sip of tea. "Many changes have come."

They both turned as Sarah opened the bedroom door and stepped into the room. Her eyes were sparkling with excitement. "I had to get up and make sure last night wasn't a dream," she said. "Rand and I talked about it after we went to bed, and we want you and John to stay with us, Morning Song. You can't go back to the Sioux. You said they didn't treat the baby or you very well. We love you and want you to become part of our family."

Morning Song swallowed hard as she visibly fought tears. "I do not wish to be burden for my friends," she said almost inaudibly. "Shoshone chief say I can stay at his encampment. But I wish to leave my son with you. Baby deserve to be accepted by whites."

Sarah nodded vigorously. "But we won't keep him without you, Morning Song. You must stay also. Rand has already gone to ask the commander for permission for you to stay. He's sure the commander will allow it. He is a very compassionate man."

Morning Song lost her battle against the tears and they slid down her cheeks noiselessly. "I must help Say-rah if I stay," she said. "And baby is very good. We try not to disturb my friends."

Sarah smiled. "There will be plenty of crying in a few months anyway. My baby will be born in two months, and Emmie's baby should arrive in May."

Morning Song looked at Emmie quickly. "You not stay here all the time? You have husband here?"

Emmie shook her head slowly. *How much should I tell Morning Song?* she wondered. The suffering on the other girl's face convinced her. She deserved the truth, she thought. "No husband. Like you, I was not really married, although I thought I was. I am staying here with my friends, just like you."

A ghost of a smile flitted across Morning Song's face. "Rand will act like he eat loco weed after all babies come."

Sarah and Emmie chuckled. "He'll survive it," Sarah said. "Now let's see about getting you some other clothes. Then we'll go see Amelia. She'll be so glad you're here."

They scrounged through Sarah's and Emmie's wardrobes before deciding on a blue flannel dress of Emmie's. It was a little too small for Emmie now, but it fit Morning Song's too thin frame loosely. They helped her bathe and dress, then arranged her hair in a coronet of braids around her head. Her moccasins were full of holes, but a pair of Sarah's boots fit fairly well. She looked like a modest young white woman with a suntan when they were finished with her.

Morning Song stared at herself in the small hand mirror and smiled in delight. She'd always wanted to be a part of Sarah's world. The snow had finally stopped, so they donned warm cloaks and bonnets, bundled the baby up, and hurried across the parade ground to Amelia's.

The house was dark when they let themselves in. Emmie noticed the fire was almost out, so she threw some more logs on it while Sarah hurried to the bedroom to check on Amelia.

"Emmie, come quickly!" Sarah called urgently from the bedroom. "The baby's coming!"

Emmie rushed to the bedroom with Morning Song close behind her. A slick sheen of sweat coated Amelia's pale face and she moaned softly. She was so pale, Emmie felt a stab of pure terror. *Help her, Lord,* she prayed silently. *Give her strength in this hour.* She took Amelia's hand. "Your baby will be here soon," she said soothingly. "You're going to be a mama today."

Amelia moaned again.

"Sarah, I'll run and get Doc Horton," Emmie said. She knew by one look at Sarah's pale face that she was in no shape to take charge. "Morning Song, would you go find me some rags and boil some water? I'll send someone to go find Jake. This must have come on suddenly after he left."

At that moment they heard the door bang and Jake rushed in with Dr. Horton close behind. "I thank God you're here," Jake said. "I didn't want to leave her alone. I kept hoping someone would stop by, but no one was out with the weather so nasty."

They all stepped out of the room so the doctor could examine her in private. Jake paced back and forth across the kitchen, pausing now and then to gaze into the bedroom. Beyond an initial look of recognition when he saw Morning Song, he withdrew into himself and said nothing to any of them.

Emmie finally took his arm. "Let's pray," she suggested.

He gave her a startled look. "You're right," he groaned as he dropped to his knees beside a kitchen chair.

Emmie knelt on one side and Sarah and Morning Song on the other.

"Lord, we know You're here with us right now," Jake said. "We know You love Amelia even more than we do. We pray that You would be with her in her hour of travail. Give her strength and endurance. Bring the baby quickly and ease her pain." He broke off with a choked sound that was half sob and half groan. He drew a shaky breath and continued. "And help us to endure watching her suffer. We leave her in Your hands, Father. In Jesus' name. Amen."

They all stayed on their knees for a few more moments, then rose as Dr. Horton came into the room. "She's in a bad way," the doctor said bluntly. "She's too weak to stand much of this and the baby is coming the wrong way. Have any of you ladies helped deliver babies before?"

Sarah and Emmie looked at each other and shook their heads.

Morning Song nodded slowly. "I help many women in my village."

Dr. Horton looked at her for a moment, then evidently satisfied with what he saw, nodded. "Wash your hands and come with me. You, too," he said to Emmie.

Morning Song and Emmie hurried to obey. They scrubbed their hands with lye soap and went into the bedroom.

"We've got to try to turn the baby," the doctor said. "Emmie, I need you to hold her down while I push on her stomach. Do you know what to do?" he asked Morning Song.

She nodded and knelt by Amelia.

Emmie thought she couldn't stand it as Amelia thrashed and cried out while Morning Song inserted her hand and began to turn the baby as gently as she could. She was trembling and dripping with perspiration by the time the doctor stood up.

"You can let her go now," he said. "Things should move along now. You did very well," he told Morning Song approvingly. "Now both of you get out of here and try to calm Jake down."

Emmie closed the door behind her with a sense of relief. Jake was beside her instantly. "How is she?" he demanded in a shaky voice.

"We got the baby turned," she said. "The doctor says it should be all right now." That wasn't exactly what he said, but Emmie hoped it was true. She washed her hands at the wash bucket, then went to the stove on shaky legs and poured a cup of coffee.

Amelia cried out behind the closed door and Jake shuddered convulsively. He sank to a chair and buried his face in his hands. "I can't stand it," he muttered.

The entry door opened and his brother rushed in. "I heard the baby is coming," Rand said. He took in the grave faces in the kitchen. "She's going to be all right, isn't she?" he asked Sarah.

Sarah leaned against him and buried her face in his chest. "The doctor thinks so now. But she's very weak."

The afternoon dragged on as they paced outside the bedroom door. Finally, Amelia cried out again, then they heard the weak, wavering cry of a newborn baby. Jake shot to his feet and looked at the bedroom door wildly. Rand stepped forward and gripped his arm. "Calm down, little brother. You won't do Amelia any good in this state."

Just then the door opened and Dr. Horton stepped through. He looked into Jake's agonized eyes and smiled reassuringly. "You have a beautiful daughter, Jake."

Jake's face was white. "How's my wife?"

"See for yourself." The doctor gestured toward the bedroom.

Jake jumped forward like he was shot out of a cannon. The rest of the family followed him eagerly. Amelia lay against the pillows with a little more color in her cheeks. A tiny face with a tuft of dark hair peeked out from under her arm. Jake sank to his knees beside his wife and daughter and stared at them with awe.

Amelia smiled up at them. "Isn't she beautiful? I'm glad we decided to name her Gabrielle. God's messenger. She really is a wonderful message from God."

"You're beautiful," Jake told her. He kissed her gently on the forehead, then turned his attention to his daughter. "She looks just like you," he said in wonder.

"Does she really?" Amelia looked up at her friends questioningly.

"Without a doubt," Rand said.

"Aren't you going to hold her, Jake?" Sarah said. "First you, then it's my turn."

Amelia lifted the baby and Jake took her awkwardly. Her blue eyes, so like Amelia's, stared up at him and he swallowed hard. After a few moments of mutual inspection, he handed the baby to Sarah.

She took her eagerly and snuggled her expertly. "Oh, Amelia, she's adorable!"

Amelia smiled and her eyes closed wearily. Emmie saw her friend's exhaustion and motioned them all out. She was just about to shut the door when Amelia opened her eyes and motioned to her to come back. "What is it, Amelia?" she said gently. "You need to get some rest."

"Thank you," Amelia said. "And thank Morning Song for me. You both saved my life. I was so surprised to see her. Tell her I want to have a long talk when I'm stronger."

Emmie smiled and smoothed Amelia's hair away from her forehead. "I'll tell her. I told you there was nothing to worry about. You're going to be here to take care of your own husband and baby."

Amelia smiled, then her eyes closed again and Emmie tiptoed out.

By the time they had all exclaimed over the baby's perfection and had taken turns holding her, it was nearly time for supper. Emmie reluctantly handed the baby to Jake, and they all bundled up to head home. Weariness slowed her steps and she lagged behind the others as they walked across the parade ground toward their tiny quarters. A figure loomed out of the shadows and she choked back a scream before she realized it was Isaac.

He fell into step beside her. "Amelia and the baby okay?"

"Yes, thank God," Emmie said fervently.

"I heard you and Morning Song were the heroines of the hour. You're a gritty little thing." His tone was admiring.

"I didn't do anything but hold her down," she told him. "Morning Song and the doctor did it all."

"Doc Horton said he had you help because he knew you wouldn't faint. He was pretty sure Sarah would. He said you have a lot of backbone."

Emmie felt a warm glow at the words. "I didn't think I could stand it," she admitted.

Isaac stopped and took her arm. "You've gotten a lot more confident in the past few weeks. I think it's because of your faith. Don't you think God wants you to put the past behind you? You gave Him your fear. Can't you give Him your past and all its hurts?" His fingers grasped her chin and he tilted her head up until he could look into her eyes. "I love you, Emmie. Can you look me in the eye and tell me you don't love me?"

Emmie tried to draw away, but his fingers under her chin were insistent. His usually smiling blue eyes were serious as he stared down at her. "I–I don't know," she said unsteadily. "I don't want to love you." She burst into tears. "I don't want to be hurt again," she sobbed.

Isaac drew her into the shelter of his arms and rested his chin on her head. "I won't hurt you, my love. From the first moment I laid eyes on you, I knew you were the one I'd been waiting for. I want to be your baby's father. I've seen the gentle, loving spirit you have. You may not want to love me, but I think you do." He drew back and tilted her chin up again. "Don't you?" He bent his head and kissed her.

As his lips touched hers, Emmie felt all her resistance melt away. She did love Isaac. She'd tried to deny it to herself, but it was true. She loved his goodness, his devotion to God, his unwavering kindness to his friends, his sense of humor, everything about him. She gave a choked sob and wound her arms around his neck as she kissed him back.

When Isaac finally drew back, he was trembling. "Does this mean you'll marry me?" he asked with a teasing smile.

Tears hung on Emmie's lashes and she brushed them away. "Yes, I'll marry you," she whispered. *How can I tell him the truth about Monroe?* she thought. *I must wait for the right time.*

He put an arm around her and led her toward the Campbell quarters. "Let's go tell everyone."

The kitchen was bustling with activity when they arrived. Morning Song was cutting up venison while Sarah peeled potatoes. Rand and Joel were putting the bread and butter out and setting the table. Emmie and Isaac stood and watched for a few moments before Sarah looked up and saw them.

"Oh," Sarah breathed. "What's happened? You look so—" She broke off as she ran out of words.

"I've finally worn down Emmie's resistance," Isaac said. "She's going to be Mrs. Lieutenant Liddle."

Sarah shrieked and dropped her potatoes on the floor. She flung her arms around Emmie and danced her around the room. "I just knew you two were meant for each other," she crowed. "I knew God would work it out."

Rand slapped Isaac on the back. "I told you to keep trying," he grinned.

Sarah gaped at her husband. "You told me to stay out of it," she said with a merry scowl.

"He thought one meddling Campbell was enough." Grinning, Isaac chucked her under the chin.

Morning Song kissed Emmie on the cheek gently. "I am happy for my sister," she said. "I pray the Lord's blessings upon your life."

Emmie was touched. "Thank you, my friend," she said, near tears.

Joel gave a disgusted shake of his head, then shook Isaac's hand.

"You won't think it's so dumb in a few years," Isaac said as he ruffled Joel's hair.

"When's the wedding?" Rand asked a few minutes later as they sat around the table eating supper.

Emmie looked hesitantly at Isaac. "We haven't discussed it yet," she said. "It's all so sudden."

"Soon," Isaac put in. "I'll talk to the chaplain. How long will it take you to get ready?"

Emmie looked at Sarah helplessly. "How long?"

"A month, at least," Sarah said. "We have to make you a dress and get the food ready."

"Today's the seventeenth of December," Isaac said. "How about we plan it for January seventeenth?"

"Make it the eleventh. That's my birthday," Rand interrupted. "I'll give you a gift on my birthday. You couldn't ask for a better gift than a new wife. The Bible says, 'Whoso findeth a wife, findeth a good thing.' "

Her head reeling from the speed of everything, Emmie nodded. As they cleaned up after supper and made plans, she felt as though it was all happening to someone else. She couldn't be this happy. It wasn't possible. She kept stealing glances at Isaac's profile in the parlor, where he talked with Rand. God was so good. He was giving her the desires of her heart, just like the Bible said. But what if Isaac didn't believe her about Monroe? What if he thought she had deceived him? Her mouth went dry. She had to tell him soon.

After he took his leave, she went to her bedroom and knelt. *Help me find the right words, Lord,* she prayed. *Help him understand.* As she snuggled under the buffalo robe, she suddenly remembered Jessica. What would her reaction be? Would she really tell Isaac her perverted version of the so-called marriage? She shivered in spite of the warmth of the buffalo robe. She must tell him tomorrow. If he heard the truth from her own lips, maybe he wouldn't believe Jessica's story.

ten

The smile on Isaac's face the next morning provoked much teasing among the men. The news of his engagement was all over the small fort encampment before he ever showed his face at officers' mess. Rooster just said, "When a woman starts draggin' a loop, there's always some man willin' to step in."

When Isaac reported for duty, Colonel Carrington congratulated him, then asked him to take a woodcutting detail out to the bend of Big Piney Creek. Although the sky was clear, the trek was slow going, with huge drifts of snow left by the blizzard. Several lines of enlisted men tramped the snow down for the horses; otherwise, the animals would have been walking through chest-high snow in some places. Isaac sat atop his horse and watched the surrounding hills for signs of trouble. The men had only felled one tree and begun to cut it up when he heard the whoops of a war band as they charged over the hill to his right.

"Take cover!" he shouted. He slid off his horse and flung himself down behind an outcropping of rock. "Lord, send help," he prayed as he saw the number of Sioux storming into the fray. The soldiers were outnumbered by at least three to one. Even with the repeating rifles some of them had, they would soon be overwhelmed. He knew the lookout on Pilot Knob could see the battle, but Carrington would need at least fifteen minutes to muster the men and come to the rescue.

❧

Morning Song had taken Joel to the sutler's store while Emmie and Sarah cleaned the kitchen. Emmie lifted her head as she heard the volley of shots in the distance. She stopped and put a hand to her pounding heart. She knew Isaac was out with the wood detail. Men were milling around the parade ground and running frantically to saddle horses. She saw Rand and Jake ride past in the first company of cavalry led by Lieutenant Fetterman. Then Colonel Carrington led a small force of mounted men out across the creek.

Sarah put her arm around Emmie. "Let's pray for the men right now," she said. The women knelt together. Emmie couldn't stop the tears from flowing. She knew she should be trusting God, but it was so hard when she knew how dangerous the situation was. They had grown accustomed to the wagon bringing in dead and wounded men daily. She just couldn't bear the thought that it may be Isaac's body brought in bristling with arrows. Now that she had finally admitted how she felt, she couldn't help fearing that he would be taken from her.

"Lord, we put our loved ones in Your hands right now," Sarah prayed. "We know You love them even more than we do. Guard them with Your might; give them insight and wisdom on how to deal with this situation. Nevertheless, not our will, but Yours, Lord. In Jesus' name we pray. Amen."

They continued to kneel beside the living room cot. Emmie felt her heart resume its normal beat and peace flooded over her. She knew He was in control, and she felt her terror ease away. She lifted her head and smiled at Sarah. "Let's go see if we can do anything for Amelia."

Sarah nodded. "I'm still worried about her. It was such a hard labor. She shouldn't be there alone."

But their fears were unfounded. Amelia was sitting up in bed with her hair brushed, a clean nightgown on, and the baby nestled in her arms. She looked up from her inspection of Baby Gabrielle as they tiptoed in the room.

"What is all the excitement about?" Amelia asked with a worried frown. "I heard the men shouting and the trumpet calling assembly."

"Nothing for you to worry about," Sarah said with a soothing hand on her friend's forehead. "Just a little skirmish with the Sioux." She frowned. "You seem a little warm. How are you feeling?"

"I'm fine," Amelia said. The frown eased off her face. Looking down at the sleeping infant, she said, "I can't believe she's really here. Isn't she the most beautiful thing you've ever seen? I just somehow knew I would have a baby girl."

Emmie leaned down beside her and touched the baby's face. "She's wonderful," she said. "You're so blessed. It's going to seem like such a long time before my baby comes now that you have her. Sarah and I will probably wear out our welcome in the first week."

"Don't count on it," Amelia said with a smile. "I can never see too much of you." She sat up in bed a little straighter and patted the side of the bed. "Sit down both of you and tell me all the fort news. Have you heard from home lately? What has Jessica been up to?"

Emmie sat on one side of the bed and Sarah pulled the cracked straight-backed chair up closer to the bed and sat down. "Well, I do have some exciting news," Emmie said with a shy smile.

"Don't tell me. Let me guess," Amelia said. She looked into Emmie's shining face for a moment. "You're engaged to Isaac."

Emmie gaped at her and Amelia burst out laughing. "I'm not a mind reader. Jake told me last night." She leaned forward and hugged Emmie. "I'm so happy for both of you. Isaac is a wonderful man."

"God is very good to me," Emmie said softly. "I just hope I don't disappoint Isaac." She stood and walked to the window. "How well do we really know someone else? I'm not very brave, you know. I'm just afraid that when Isaac gets to know me better, he'll wish he had married someone else. And how will he react when he knows I was never really married to Monroe?"

Sarah stepped quickly to the window and turned Emmie around to face her. "You're not to think like that anymore," she told her firmly. "God has not given us a spirit of fear, but of power and a sound mind. Remember? Isaac is no fool. He knows you well enough now to know you aren't a loose woman."

Emmie smiled, then nodded. "I'll try to keep that in mind."

"When is the wedding?" Amelia asked.

"January eleventh. It's Rand's birthday. He'll give me away."

Amelia's face brightened. "I'll be back to normal by then. Too bad Gabrielle won't be bigger. She could be in the bridal party."

Emmie caressed the baby's face. "She'll be there and that's good enough for me. You certainly had us frightened."

Amelia sighed and adjusted her blankets. "I had some kind of silly premonition that I was going to die. I'm just so thankful it's over and we're both all right."

Sarah took her friend's hand. "We wouldn't let anything happen to you. You're too special to us."

Amelia squeezed Sarah's hand. "Sometimes God decrees otherwise," she said softly.

Sarah gave one final pat to Amelia's hand, then leaned over and kissed the baby. "We'd better be getting back. We'll come back and bring you some nice soup for lunch. Do you need anything else before we go?"

Amelia shook her head. "I think I'll take a little nap while Gabrielle is sleeping." She snuggled down into the blankets.

"I'll put her in the cradle so you can rest better." Emmie gently took the baby and placed her in her cradle beside the bed. Jake had spent many evenings carving a woodland scene on it. Bunnies frolicked among flowers in a meadow, beautifully done. She tucked the blankets around Gabrielle, then followed Sarah out of the room.

They checked the fire and made sure it had enough wood before they hurried across the parade ground toward the sutler's store. They'd been gone nearly an hour. Any news of the fate of the wood detail would be known at the store.

The store teemed with soldiers and other wives. Sarah saw Frances Grummond standing by the counter. Frances waved and immediately made her way toward them. She clutched at Emmie's arm and burst into tears.

"I'm so frightened," she sobbed. "Lieutenant Smith says Fetterman took a company of infantry and one of cavalry to the relief of the wood detail, while Colonel Carrington and George went with a small detail to cut off the Indians' retreat. But the scouts say our men were heavily outnumbered. At least one officer has been killed and several more men wounded. No one knows who yet."

The lump in Emmie's throat threatened to choke her. *Please keep our men safe,* she prayed silently. Sarah invited Frances back to their quarters to await any further news. The day passed in fitful periods of conversation. A pall of fear hung over all three women as they tried to keep up their spirits. They sang hymns, took meals to Amelia, worked with Joel on his studies, and above all, prayed. Finally, about nine o'clock in the evening, the bugle sounded the return of the troops. They hastily threw on cloaks and hats and hurried across the parade ground to greet the returning soldiers.

Emmie watched fearfully as the men filed through. Their faces were strained and red from the cold wind. Sarah cried out in relief as she spotted Rand, then Jake. Emmie strained her eyes in the dark, trying to see a familiar set of shoulders. Where was Isaac? She whispered another prayer and scanned the melee again. There! There he was. She felt tears of thanksgiving well up in her eyes as he turned and saw her. He smiled and waved. The men couldn't speak with them for some time, but at least they were safe.

"No-o-o!"

Emmie turned at the drawn out wail. Mrs. DuBois screamed and beat at her daughter's restraining arms that held her from rushing to the ambulance.

"Major DuBois must be the officer who was killed," Sarah whispered.

Emmie wanted to go offer her condolences, but she knew Jessica wouldn't welcome them. At least not yet. It was hard to believe that the strong, vibrant Major had been felled by a Sioux arrow.

Isaac was exhausted and didn't stay long when he dropped in later that evening, so Emmie had no chance to talk to him about Monroe. It was only by God's grace that all the men hadn't been killed, Isaac told her before he left. If the Sioux had managed to surround them, all would have been lost. She fretted as she lay in bed again that night until she reminded herself that God was in control. He had taken care of Isaac, and He would take care of her.

❧

The next day, Sarah and Emmie went to pay their respects to Mrs. DuBois and Jessica. Emmie's heart pounded and her mouth was dry as she followed Sarah across the parade ground to the Major's quarters. Jessica was sure to have heard the news of the engagement by now. How would she react? Emmie had not had an opportunity to tell Isaac about her "marriage."

Mrs. DuBois's striker answered the door and ushered them into the parlor. Most of the officers employed "strikers," an enlisted man who worked for them as a servant on their off-duty hours for a small compensation. Emmie had asked why Rand hadn't done the same instead of taking in a homeless waif like her. It was probably more expensive to pay for her expenses than to employ a striker. But Sarah had told her that Rand thought Sarah needed the company more than the physical help.

Jessica, sitting alone and staring out the window, looked up as they entered the room. Her eyes, swollen from crying, narrowed as she saw Emmie. "What do you want?" she burst out. "Did you come here to gloat? You have everything you want."

Emmie flinched. "We just want you to know how sorry we are about your father. I would like to be your friend, Jessica.

Not your enemy. I never meant to hurt you."

Her face flushing with rage, Jessica rose and advanced toward them. "Get out!" she hissed. "I don't want your condolences and I certainly don't need your friendship."

Emmie swallowed hard and put out a trembling hand to Jessica. "I've been praying for you, Jessica. I don't know what hurt drives you so, but God does. And He can heal your pain, if you let Him."

Jessica's eyes filled with tears, but then her face hardened and she flushed a deeper red. "Get out!" She advanced toward them. "Get out, get out, get out!" She screamed the words at them. "I don't need your pity!"

Emmie and Sarah backed away hastily. "We truly are sorry," Sarah said as they slipped back out through the door. "We really didn't come just to be polite."

As the door shut in their faces, Emmie and Sarah looked at each other. Sarah was pale, Emmie noticed, and she was sure she looked just as ravaged as her friend did.

"You know, I think you have a lot of insight," Sarah said a few minutes later as they had a cup of tea back in their own kitchen. "I never really thought about why Jessica is like she is. There must be some hidden pain in her life that has shaped her. We really should pray for her. God could heal her."

They knelt beside their chairs and asked God to send peace and a sense of His love to Jessica. Instead of anger, they both felt a sense of compassion for Jessica DuBois. God alone knew what she needed to be whole.

The next day Emmie spent most of the morning making pies and bread. She tried a recipe of Mrs. Horton's for mincemeat pie and decided to take a piece to Amelia. Morning Song was at the Indian encampment, so Sarah decided to accompany her.

The women bundled up in warm cloaks and hurried toward Amelia's quarters. The weather had been frigid and the wind snatched their breath away as soon as they stepped outside. As they approached Jake and Amelia's small cabin, they heard the baby's wail. The infant sounded frantic, and Emmie hastened her steps. What could be wrong with little Gabrielle?

They didn't bother to knock, but opened the door and hurried to the bedroom, where the baby lay shrieking in her bed. Amelia lay on the floor beside the bed, one arm reaching toward the cradle where her tiny daughter lay.

"Quick, help me get her back into bed," Sarah said as she knelt beside their friend. She grasped Amelia's shoulders and Emmie lifted her legs.

"She's burning up!" Emmie said as she touched Amelia's skin. The women managed to lift her into the bed. "You take care of the baby and I'll fetch Dr. Horton."

Sarah hurried to pick up the baby as Emmie flew out the door and across the parade ground. By the time she and the doctor returned, Sarah had managed to calm the baby with a cloth dipped in sugar water. The baby was sucking on it vigorously and making mewing sounds of contentment.

Dr. Horton frowned when he felt the heat radiating off Amelia's body. He quickly put his stethoscope to her chest and listened intently. Amelia muttered incoherently and moved restlessly in the bed.

"What is it?" Sarah asked anxiously as the doctor put his instruments away.

"Pneumonia, I'm afraid," Dr. Horton said. "Her condition is very grave. We must try to reduce the fever. You need to sponge her down with tepid water. She won't like it, but it must be done."

Emmie nodded. "I'll do it while you take care of the baby," she told Sarah. Sarah nodded. "When Morning Song gets back, we can send her to the sutler's store for some tinned milk."

Emmie warmed a pan of water to lukewarm and began to sponge Amelia's body. Wring, wipe, wring, wipe. Over and over, Emmie wiped the damp cloth over Amelia's body. After an hour, she felt as though her arms would fall off. But still Amelia drifted in and out of consciousness, calling for Jake and Baby Gabrielle. Morning Song and Sarah peeked in several times. Gabrielle was fretful, so finally Sarah asked Morning Song if she would mind acting as a wet nurse for the baby. After nursing the baby, Morning Song tucked her into her bed. The doctor checked back in also, but his expression grew more grave every time he saw Amelia's unchanged condition.

Around noon, Morning Song slipped in behind Emmie. She had a cup of steaming liquid in her hands. "I wish to try some Sioux medicine. It is from the bark of a tree you call white oak."

Emmie lifted Amelia's head and shoulders onto her lap while Morning Song spooned the steaming liquid into her mouth. Some ran out the corners of her mouth, but she managed to swallow some. Emmie wiped Amelia's mouth and eased her back against the pillows.

"I wish Jake would get back," Sarah said as the afternoon wore on. "I'm so afraid."

Amelia moaned and both women knelt beside her bed. She opened her eyes and Emmie noticed how bright and blue they looked against the pure white of her face. Those blue eyes shone with love and a strange joy. Emmie swallowed hard and fought a rising sense of panic as Amelia smiled at someone just past Emmie's shoulder. Emmie almost turned around to look, but she knew there was no one there.

"Tell Jake I'll be waiting for him," Amelia whispered. "I'm sorry I have to leave him alone."

"No, no," Sarah said. "Don't talk like that. Jake will be here soon and you'll be fine."

Amelia shook her head. "You must be strong, Sarah," she whispered. "Help Jake all you can and tell him I love him." She coughed violently, then lay gasping for air. She looked again at a spot just to the side of Emmie, stretched out her arms, and closed her eyes. She gave one last little sigh, a strange little hiccup, and her chest grew still. Baby Gabrielle wailed suddenly as though she somehow knew her mother was gone.

"No!" Sarah wailed. She tried to pull Amelia to a sitting position, but she was limp and unresponsive.

Emmie took Sarah by the shoulders and pulled her close. She swallowed hard past the tears burning in her throat. How could this be? She leaned her forehead against Sarah's head and closed her eyes as Sarah cried out in sudden comprehension of the loss of her best friend. Morning Song hurried to tend to the crying baby. Emmie heard her clucking noises of comfort through the dull veil of grief that squeezed her heart. "She's gone," she whispered against Sarah's hair. "But we know she's with Jesus."

"She can't be dead," Sarah said numbly. "She can't be. We've always been there for each other. This can't be true. Call the doctor." But the words were said without any real conviction. They clung together for several unbelieving minutes.

"We must pray," Emmie choked out. They both turned toward the bed. Emmie picked up Amelia's still hand and laid her lips against it. Sarah laid one hand on her friend's brow for the last time. "Oh Father, we hardly know what to pray because of the grief that overwhelms us. We pray for strength to see all of us through the coming days and nights. We ask especially for Your guiding hands to lead us through this valley of death. Jake and little Gabrielle are going to need Your love and mercy in these dark days even more than we do. We know that our sister is in Your presence and we thank You for that. Let us sense Your loving arms as well."

They stayed in the same position for a few moments. Emmie felt a warmth steal through her limbs and a strange comfort enveloped her. She felt as though God was right beside her in a real and physical way. She could almost sense His touch on her shoulder. She looked at Sarah's white face and held out her hand.

Sarah shook her head. "I want to stay here for just a few

minutes," she said with a pleading look. "I just want to remember the good times we had when we were growing up." Her words were choked with tears. "I still can't believe she's gone." Emmie touched her gently on the shoulder, then left her alone with Amelia.

Morning Song was in the kitchen with little Gabrielle. Emmie put water on to boil for some tea, then sat wearily beside Morning Song. Young John played happily on the floor with some wooden blocks. "I don't know how to tell Jake," Emmie whispered.

Jake. Emmie could only imagine the pain he would feel. And he had a new baby to care for. Of course they would all help, but it was still a huge responsibility to raise a child alone. Emmie gulped as she thought about the situation. Her promise to Amelia. She'd promised Amelia she would marry Jake and care for Gabrielle if anything happened. *Surely Amelia wouldn't expect me to keep a promise like that now that I've found Isaac,* she told herself. She bit her lip and blinked back more tears. Just when life had seemed so perfect, everything fell apart. How could any of them even look forward to the wedding when Amelia was gone?

The day dragged by somehow. Morning Song took the children home to Sarah's, while Sarah and Emmie washed Amelia's cold, still body and dressed her in her favorite Sunday dress, the violet one that deepened the color of her eyes. Emmie couldn't bear the thought of those extraordinary eyes never widening in wonder again. Sarah combed and dressed her friend's long dark hair one last time as her tears gently bathed Amelia's white but still beautiful face. As the sad news traveled around the post, several ladies dropped by with whispers of condolences and offerings of food.

The bugle finally sounded the men's return to the fort, but it was nearly an hour before they heard the heavy tread of the men on the front porch. Isaac and Rand each held Jake's arms as they practically carried him through the door. His face was slack and glazed with disbelief and an overwhelming grief.

All three men bore signs of the tears they'd shed. Isaac's eyes were full of sorrow as they met Emmie's, and he opened his arms to her. Sarah uttered a tiny cry and flew into Rand's arms and they all wept together as Jake stumbled toward the room where his wife lay.

Moments later, they heard his harsh sobs as he sank to the floor beside Amelia. Emmie's eyes filled with tears again. Isaac pulled her closer and rested his chin on the top of her head as she sobbed against his chest. His shirt smelled of cold air and the warm musk of his male scent. She felt loved and comforted in the circle of his arms with his breath warm on her face. But the grief and aloneness poor Jake must be feeling!

After a little while, the four of them tiptoed into the bedroom to be with Jake. His sobs had stilled, but his fingers still traced the contours of Amelia's face. Rand put his hand on his brother's shoulder.

"I never got to say good-bye," Jake choked. "How could she leave without saying good-bye?"

Sarah knelt beside him. "Her last words were for you. She said, 'Tell Jake I'll be waiting for him. Tell him I love him.'"

Jake groaned and buried his face in his hands. His shoulders shook with the intensity of his grief. After a few moments, he lifted his head. "Where's the baby? Is she all right?"

"She's fine," Emmie said. "Morning Song took her to our house along with John and Joel."

"I want her. She's all I have left of Amelia now."

"I'll go get her," Emmie said.

"The wind is terrible. Let me go," Isaac said.

Emmie shook her head. "I want to. I'll be fine." She hurriedly wrapped her cloak about her and stepped out into the wind-whipped snow. She was numb from the emotions of the day as she hurried across the parade ground. The wind stung her cheeks and the prickle of feeling brought a new wave of grief. How would they all bear this?

Morning Song looked up as Emmie stumbled into the parlor. Little Gabrielle and John slept contentedly on the cot. Joel dozed with his head against Morning Song's knee. Emmie looked at the baby, sleeping so peacefully. Her heart clenched with love for the motherless mite. Amelia would have been such a wonderful mother. Now little Gabrielle would never know the lovely person who had given her birth. Tears stung her eyes as the baby stirred and opened blue eyes so very like her mother's.

"Jake is back and wants to see the baby," Emmie said.

She knelt beside the cot and gently bundled the blankets around the baby. She lifted the baby into her arms and looked at Morning Song for a moment. "He's taking it very hard."

Morning Song nodded. "I knew it would be so. When one is cut, the other bleeds. I should come, too?"

Emmie shook her head. "You stay with the boys. There's no sense in making them come out in this cold. When we get back, maybe you could go over and feed her."

"I come."

There was a thread of emotion Emmie didn't recognize in Morning Song's voice. The Indian woman was so stoical most of the time. It was hard to guess what she felt and how strongly Amelia's death was affecting her. With a last glance at her friend, she pulled the blanket over Gabrielle's face and tucked her under her cloak for added warmth. The wind caught the door out of her fingers, but Morning Song was behind her to grab it and pull it shut.

Jake was waiting at the door when she stomped the snow off her feet on the porch. He took the bundled baby out of her arms as soon as she extricated her from under the cloak. With tender hands, he pulled back the blankets and gazed into his daughter's tiny face. She yawned and opened her blue eyes.

"You look so much like your mama," Jake whispered. "Thank God." He pulled her close, then went to the bedroom and shut the door.

Emmie sank wearily onto the cot in the parlor. Isaac put a hand on her shoulder and squeezed gently.

"We'll get through this. God is here and in control."

Emmie nodded. She knew that it was so. But why would God allow such sorrow to come to them? She didn't know if she would ever understand.

eleven

The next few days sped by as the entire fort rallied around the Campbell family. Ladies brought in mountains of food and the men stood around ill at ease but unwilling to leave. The grave site had to be prepared, no easy task in the hard, frozen soil.

The day of the funeral dawned clear and cold. December twentieth, just five days before Christmas. The wind wasn't as fierce as usual, which was a mercy from God, Sarah told Emmie. Jake was insistent that the baby be at the service, although she was much too tiny to be out in the weather. Emmie bundled her carefully, then followed Sarah and Rand to the little chapel. Isaac was waiting for her outside the door.

"I've been praying for you all morning," he whispered as he opened the door for her. "For all of you." He squeezed her hand gently.

Emmie nodded gratefully. "We're going to need God's grace today," she said. "Rand was at Jake's all night. Morning Song, too. She insisted she should be the one to go, since she is feeding the baby. Poor little John looks so bewildered. He doesn't understand what his mama is doing with that other baby all the time."

She eased onto the bench beside Sarah and Rand. Jake sat on the other side of his brother. He stared down at his hands with such a look of suffering on his face that Emmie's eyes filled with fresh tears. She ached to comfort his grief somehow, but she knew only God could give him the peace he needed. She offered a quick prayer for the minister as he made his way to the pulpit. *Give him the words that will comfort Jake,* she prayed. Isaac held her hand and the warm press of his fingers gave her strength.

Reverend Howard cleared his throat nervously as he glanced around at the packed building. The entire garrison had turned out to see Amelia put to rest. "Today is a day of mourning for us gathered here to pay our final respects to Amelia Campbell." He leaned forward slightly over the pulpit. "But I say to all of you that it is a day of great rejoicing as well."

Jake glanced up sharply with a frown.

"No one could speak with Amelia for long without knowing about the great love she held for her Savior. If she could speak to us today, she would tell us not to mourn but to rejoice with her that she now sees her Jesus face to face." He opened his Bible. "I want to read a passage that meant a great deal to me when my own beloved mother passed away. Listen to Psalm Fifteen and see if you agree with me that this so perfectly describes the Amelia Campbell we all knew and loved. 'Lord, who shall abide in thy tabernacle? who shall dwell in thy holy hill? He that walketh uprightly, and worketh righteousness, and speaketh the truth in his heart. He that backbiteth not with his tongue, nor doeth evil to his neighbour, nor taketh up a reproach against his neighbour. In whose eyes a vile person is contemned; but he honoureth them that fear the Lord. He that sweareth to his own hurt, and changeth not. He that putteth not out his money to usury, nor taketh reward against the innocent. He that doeth these things shall never be moved.' In Psalm 116:15 we are told, 'Precious in the sight of the Lord is the death of his saints.' This is not a punishment from God but a reward for our dear sister." He shut his Bible and looked out over the crowd. "Some of you may wish to tell about how Amelia demonstrated her love for her God in your own lives."

He sat down and the chapel was silent, then one by one people stood and told of kindnesses that Amelia had done. Tears rained down Emmie's cheeks as she listened to the outpouring of love. Jake sobbed audibly when one soldier told how he had popped a button on his coat while carrying in a load of wood for Amelia, and she insisted on sewing it back on and then given him some tea and buttered bread.

"I'll never forget as long as I live listening to that little gal pray for the food," he said. "I was afeered to look over my shoulder I was that sure I'd see God Hisself standing behind me."

The chapel was silent for a few moments, then Reverend Howard stood again. "The Bible tells that life is but a vapor and quickly passes away. We know not when God will call us home. We can only hope to live each day to His glory and make a difference with our fellow man. I think we can all heartily agree that Amelia Campbell lived her life to the fullest. She loved her family and she loved her fellow man. I pray that each one of us can impact lives the way she did."

He prayed briefly for God's sustaining grace to be shown to the family and the service was concluded. As Emmie, clinging to Isaac's arm, followed the procession to the grave, her heart was lighter than she would have dreamed possible. Someday she would also face her Savior. She could only imagine the joy Amelia was feeling at this moment. How could she mourn when she thought of her friend's unimaginable bliss? A glance at Jake's face showed he did not share her thoughts. Grief was etched deeply in his face as he carried his daughter through the ankle-deep snow.

The service at graveside was brief, just the traditional ashes to ashes, dust to dust eulogy. As they hurried home through the increasing wind, Emmie felt a sense of uneasiness as she followed Jake's broad back. He seemed hard and angry. She knew he blamed God. When the minister had tried to offer words of comfort, he had turned away with a harsh, "Don't talk to me of God's grace and mercy. My wife is dead and my daughter is motherless." She had never expected an attitude like that from Jake. Amelia had said he had a strong faith. *But a blow like this could shake the strongest faith,* Emmie thought. Best to leave it in God's hands. He would show Jake He was still there for him.

"Emmie, would you mind coming in a moment?" Jake said as they reached his quarters. "I need to talk to you for a minute."

"Of course," she said and followed him inside after a quick wave at the rest of the Campbell clan. She hung her cloak on a hook in the hall and hurried to the kitchen to boil some water for tea. She was cold clear through and knew Jake had to be as well. Jake put little Gabrielle on the bed and sat at the kitchen table while Emmie rummaged through the open shelves for some teacups. He sat silently while she finished preparing the tea. She glanced over at him once or twice and felt a little intimidated by his grim look.

"Sugar?" she asked. He shook his head and took the steaming cup. She dropped sugar in her own cup and sat beside him at the table.

"You aren't going to like what I have to say," he said abruptly. "I need your help."

Emmie smiled at him in relief. Was that all this was about? "You know I'll help in any way I can," she said. "I loved Amelia, too. I know it will be hard to take care of Gabrielle by yourself."

"I need more than just occasional help," Jake said. "Gabrielle needs a full-time mother. I don't want her growing up shifted from place to place like a homeless puppy."

Emmie's smile faltered. "You want me to take her? Don't you want her to live with you?"

"I wouldn't give my daughter up for anything," Jake said with a scowl. "She's the only important thing in my life. I don't want you to take her to live with you. I want you to live here with me and take care of her."

"Jake, I would do anything I could to help, but I can't stay here alone with you. The entire fort would talk."

"Not if we were married. I want you to honor your promise to Amelia."

The words hammered into her brain and Emmie sat back as though from a blow. Honor her promise? She couldn't marry

Jake! She was going to marry Isaac. Kind, loving Isaac who was waiting for her at Sarah's. She shook her head. "You can't be serious. You know I'm going to marry Isaac."

"You made a promise. Amelia expects you to keep it. I expect you to keep it. I know you are a woman of your word and Gabrielle needs a mother. You needn't worry about me bothering you or expecting anything else from you except to take care of my daughter. I'll never love another woman like I loved Amelia. You'll take care of Gabrielle, fix my meals, and take care of the house. That's all. You and the baby can have the bedroom. I'll sleep on the cot in the parlor."

He stared at her fiercely as he said the words. The stern look on his face seemed to dare her to contradict his demand. Emmie swallowed hard. What should she do? Didn't he know how unreasonable his demand was? Did he really expect her to give up her life and future with the man she loved to be an unloved nursemaid and housekeeper? *You made a promise,* a voice inside her head whispered. *A Christian honors her word.*

Jake stood up abruptly. "I know this is a shock, so I'm going to leave you and run over to talk to the colonel for a little while. You think it over. I know you'll do the right thing."

The right thing? This was supposed to be the right thing? Emmie stared at his back as he strode out the door. How could he ask such a thing of her? What should she do?

A timid knock at the door broke into her confused thoughts. "Come in," she called. She was relieved to see Morning Song slip inside and close the door gently.

"I have come to feed baby," Morning Song said.

"Gabrielle is still asleep," Emmie told her. "Would you like some tea while we wait for her to wake up?"

Morning Song nodded. "Tea sound good. Winter wind very bad." She looked into Emmie's eyes. "My friend is not happy. This place is sad for you."

Emmie nodded. "Yes, but that's not the only problem. I don't know what to do about Jake." She stood and put the kettle on the woodstove, then sat down and clenched her hands in her lap. "I made a promise to Amelia. One that I never thought I would have to keep."

"Promise very important. My father say if a brave cannot keep his word in the camp, do not trust him in battle with the enemy."

"But what if keeping the promise will ruin the person's life?" Emmie's eyes were full of unshed tears as she gazed pleadingly at Morning Song.

"Sometimes promise is hard, but man's word is how man is measured. Promise should never be made without thought. Remember what minister say today? About keeping oath even when it hurts?"

"I made the promise without thinking," Emmie admitted. "But it was only to ease Amelia's agitation. I never expected to have to keep it." The kettle began to whistle and she went to the stove and poured the boiling water into the teapot and brought it to the table.

Morning Song watched her prepare the tea for a moment. "What is promise?" she asked. She touched Emmie's hand softly. "God will help you keep it."

"Several weeks ago Amelia was distressed and convinced she wouldn't live through childbirth. She knew I was also expecting a child and was alone. So she asked me and Jake to marry so I could care for her baby and Jake. Then me and my baby would be provided for as well. Now Jake expects me to honor that promise." A strange look Emmie couldn't identify darkened Morning Song's features, then was gone as she listened to Emmie. Was it anger? Dismay?

Morning Song nodded slowly. "Your friend care for you even when she is afraid. I see her thoughts." Morning Song took a sip of tea, then set it down carefully. "You must honor your promise. A vow is most important when most hard."

Emmie sighed. "What about Isaac? I made a promise to him, too."

"Promise to Amelia come first, is that not right?"

She nodded. "But I love Isaac. I've been so happy these

past few days, happier than I've ever been!"

"I see this happiness. But there is still this promise you make."

The baby whimpered in the bedroom and both women looked up. Morning Song rose to her feet. "You must pray to God to show you the choice you must make. Then you must be strong enough to follow His command." Leaving Emmie with her thoughts, she turned and went into the bedroom.

Everyone expected her to be strong, but she wasn't! How could she turn her back on her love for Isaac? Emmie rose and took her cloak from the hook by the stove. She would talk to Sarah and Rand. They would know what to do. "I'm going now," she called to Morning Song. She didn't wait for an answer but hurried out into the driving wind.

The wind took her breath away, and she had to battle to stay on her feet across the parade ground. Her bonnet lifted from her head for a moment before she yanked it down and tied it firmly in place. Drifts of snow were beginning to pile up against the steps as she hurried onto the porch.

Sarah was curled up with a quilt and a magazine on the cot by the fire. She looked up as Emmie came into the parlor. "Your face is so red! You shouldn't be out in this wind. Come join me under this quilt."

Emmie threw off her cloak and hung it by the fireplace, then dove under the quilt. Even with the fire going full blast, the heat couldn't keep up with the wind, and the room was chilly. Her teeth chattered as she nestled close to Sarah.

"You are frozen," Sarah scolded as she wrapped the quilt tightly around Emmie. "Where have you been? I expected you back long ago."

"Jake wanted to talk to me."

"All this time? What did he want?"

Emmie drew her legs up under the quilt and leaned against the wall behind her. "How important do you think a promise is?"

"Very important. That's why I try not to make any promises. I don't want to break my word. Papa was always very careful before he gave his word to someone. He said a man is only as good as his word. Why? Did Jake want you to promise him something?"

"I made a promise to Amelia before she died. It didn't seem important at the time, just a way of setting her mind at ease. She thought she was going to die."

"She never told me that! When was this?" Sarah asked.

"Several weeks ago when she wasn't feeling well. She asked me to give her my word that if anything happened to her I would marry Jake and take care of him and the baby."

Sarah sat up straight. "Jake would never go for that! He would never let someone else make such an important decision for him. Not even Amelia."

"He agreed before she ever asked me. And now he wants me to keep that promise."

Sarah was silenced for a moment. "I have to admit I'm shocked. But that was before you and Isaac were engaged. Amelia would never expect you to keep a promise like that now."

"I've been thinking about it, and I think she would. When she heard about my engagement after Gabrielle was born, she said it was a good thing she made it through the birth all right so I wouldn't have to keep my promise to her. And Jake expects me to honor it now. He wants me to marry him and take care of Gabrielle." She smiled a crooked smile, though she was near tears. "He says the baby and I can sleep in the bedroom and he'll sleep on the cot. I wouldn't have to worry about any demands from him. Just take care of Gabrielle, cook, and clean."

"That's abominable! Does he just expect you to give up a full life with Isaac to become some kind of glorified nanny?" Sarah's voice rose in her agitation.

Emmie sighed again. "I know. I've been telling myself the same things for the past two hours. But I keep coming back to the fact that I promised Amelia. Doesn't God expect us to keep our word?"

Sarah wilted. "Yes," she admitted in a small voice. Then she brightened. "But you are free from the promise if Jake will release you."

"He won't," Emmie said with finality. "I don't know how I'm going to tell Isaac."

The front door burst open as Rand and Isaac came in stomping snow from their boots. Rand slammed the door shut against the wind. He glanced from Sarah to Emmie, then bent to kiss his wife. "I'm cold clear down to my socks," he said. "Any stew left?"

"It's on the stove. I'll get it." Sarah scrambled from beneath the quilt and started toward the kitchen. "Uh, why don't you help me get it ready, Rand?" she said with a side-long look at Emmie.

Rand looked surprised, but he followed her into the kitchen.

Isaac grinned. "Looks like Sarah wanted to leave us alone," he said as he sat beside Emmie on the cot. "She must have thought we wanted to do some spoonin'." He slipped an arm around her and pulled her close.

Emmie sighed and nestled in the crook of his arm. She turned her face up to him and he bent his head. As his lips found hers, Emmie closed her eyes and kissed him back with all the love in her heart. This might be the last time she felt his arms around her. She smelled the clean, crisp cold on his jacket mingled with the good scent of horse and hay. This moment would have to last the rest of her life. This one moment she could know how it felt to be embraced by a man who really loved her, one she loved with her whole being.

Isaac's arms tightened at her ardent response. He grinned as he drew back moments later. "Are you sure we can't get married sooner?" he asked.

Emmie swallowed hard and began to tremble. How could she tell him?

Isaac noticed her darkened look. "What's wrong?" he asked.

Emmie clenched her hands in her lap and silently prayed for strength. She knew she couldn't throw away everything she had ever wanted in her own strength. "I must tell you something and I don't know how," she began.

Isaac frowned. "If it's about how that no good Monroe committed bigamy, don't bother. Jessica gave me some perverted version of it, but I knew it wasn't true. Rand had already told me about it."

Emmie was glad to delay the awful news for a moment. "Rand told you? When?"

"This morning after Jessica's little bombshell. I knew she was lying, of course, but Rand told me how Monroe had deceived you." He clenched his fists. "If he weren't already dead, I'd make sure he paid for his treachery."

Emmie smiled slightly at his fierce tone, then sighed again. "That's not what I have to tell you," she said softly. "It's much worse."

"Just say it," Isaac prompted. "I love you and nothing will change that."

"I love you, too. That's what makes this so hard." Emmie looked into his dear blue eyes and her own filled with tears at the blow she must give him. "I made a promise to Amelia, one I never expected to have to keep."

Isaac smiled in relief. "I would be glad to take her baby and love her. But I doubt that Jake would allow it."

"That's only part of it," Emmie said. "Just let me finish. Amelia thought she wouldn't survive childbirth several weeks ago. This was before you and I were engaged, before I would admit even to myself how much I loved you. She asked me to give her my word that if something happened to her I would take care of the baby and marry Jake."

The only sound for a moment was the crackling of the fire and the banging of pots in the kitchen. Isaac just stared at her as all the color drained from his face. "You promised to marry Jake?"

Emmie nodded. "And he intends to hold me to my promise."

She took Isaac's hand in a desperate grip. "But I love you! What should I do?" In her heart she knew what she must do, but she prayed that he could find some way out for them both.

Isaac was silent and pain darkened his face, then he pulled his hand away and stood up. "You must honor your promise to Amelia," he said. "Only Jake could release you from it." He pulled on his greatcoat and went out the door without another word.

As soon as the door slammed shut, Rand strode into the room. "I don't know what that brother of mine has in his head, but I intend to have a talk with him," he said. "He can't ruin both your lives like this. I know he's grieving, but he just isn't thinking clearly. Don't lose hope until I can get to him." He patted Emmie's hand as the tears slipped down her cheeks. "Why don't the three of us spend some time with our Heavenly Father about this matter. We can trust Him to work things out for the best."

The three of them knelt by the cot. Emmie let her tears flow unchecked while she listened to Rand's deep voice as he prayed for guidance and God's intervention. As they rose several minutes later, she felt strong enough to do whatever the Lord deemed right. If she had to honor her promise, she felt sure the Lord would care for her even in the midst of a loveless marriage. There could be joy in serving Jake. She had always liked and respected him. She'd even envied Amelia and Sarah because of the fine husbands they had. At least there would be peace in doing God's will.

"We'll let God talk to Jake first," Rand said. "Then I'll see what he has to say. You get some rest. Things will look different tomorrow."

twelve

Isaac's thoughts were in turmoil as he strode across the windswept parade ground. His first inclination was to find Jake and shake some sense into him, but he didn't want to do anything rash. Jake wasn't thinking past his grief. "I need to pray," Isaac muttered to himself. "I need a quiet place to turn this over to God."

The small chapel at the other end of the parade ground beckoned, and he wrapped his greatcoat around him tightly and bent into the wind. The chapel was dark and cold as he shoved the door closed against the push of the gale. He lit a lantern by the door and carried it with him to the kneeling bench at the front of the chapel. As he sank to his knees on the cold wooden floorboards, he felt a sense of relief that he could turn it all over to the Lord.

His heart felt bruised and broken, and he didn't try to hide his pain from God. "Help me to understand this and deal with it if it truly is Your will, Lord," he prayed. "And be with Emmie. I know she feels the pain as I do. Help us both to follow You no matter what the consequences are." He stayed on his knees a few minutes longer, then rose and blew out the lantern. He would leave it in God's hands. He'd always told God that he wouldn't marry against His will. If it meant he wouldn't marry at all, so be it. He closed the door gently behind him and headed toward the officers' quarters. If the opportunity arose, maybe God would give him the right words to say to reach Jake. He knew his friend was hurting or he wouldn't be doing this thing. Tomorrow was a new day and God was in control.

❧

Isaac woke the next morning with a heavy heart as he remembered the events of the night before. *I'm not going to worry about it,* he told himself as he pulled on his boots and strapped his saber to his belt. Reveille was already sounding as he strode toward the stables after bolting down some hardtack in the mess hall. He saddled Buck, his buckskin gelding, and made it to the parade ground just in time for boots and saddles. He was on guard duty for the wood detail. He caught a glimpse of Rand ahead, with Jake trailing behind several other soldiers. If the Lord put the right circumstances in his way, perhaps he would get a chance to talk to Jake.

There had been so many skirmishes with the Sioux lately that the guard detail numbered near ninety men to protect the wood detail. The detail followed the river, then veered off on the trail to the Pinery cutting area. They had gone only a hundred yards or so when he heard a man in front of him yell as an arrow whistled by his ear. Rand shouted for the men to form the corral formation, and Isaac raced to form a protective circle with the other soldiers. He saw Indians massed on the hills all around and sighed in relief as he heard the picket on Pilot Hill blow the signal that told the fort there were many Indians. Relief would come from the fort soon. They just had to hold on.

ৡ

Emmie heard the signal from Pilot Hill and then the sound of the bugle calling men together, but she tried not to worry. It was an almost everyday occurrence lately. A few minutes later she heard the boom of the mountain howitzer. Joel looked up at the sound, but it, too, was almost commonplace these days. The Sioux feared the "gun that shoots twice" and almost always scattered after its use. She washed and dried the dishes while Sarah dusted and made the beds. Joel carried in wood for the fire, then ran off to play with Jimmy Carrington.

Emmie was deep in her thoughts when a knock at the door startled her. "I'll get it," she called to Sarah. Morning Song had gone to care for Baby Gabrielle first thing this morning, and she wouldn't knock anyway, so Emmie wondered who could be out this morning as she hurried to the door.

Frances Grummond's tear-stained face peered out of a fur bonnet. "Oh, Emmie, I'm so frightened," she sobbed as Emmie pulled her inside and Sarah hovered consolingly. "George volunteered to go to the rescue of the wood detail and I have such an uncanny dread on my soul. He was almost killed two weeks ago. Would you go with me to Mrs. Wands'? The other ladies are gathered there, too."

"Of course we will," Emmie said, her heart sinking. Isaac, Rand, and Jake were all with the wood detail, she knew. "Would you like some tea first?"

"No, no. I just need to be with someone. Could we go now?" Frances' voice broke as she wrung her hands.

Sarah and Emmie grabbed their cloaks and bonnets and followed Frances outside. The wind still whistled, but a weak, watery sunshine brightened the day. Frances' baby was due in just a few weeks and Emmie worried that the strain would bring on her friend's labor. She sent up a quick prayer for Frances.

The assembled ladies looked up when Emmie, Sarah, and Frances entered the Wands' parlor. Mrs. Carrington hurried to take Frances in her arms. "My dear, don't fret so. There is no more cause for concern than usual. We both heard my husband tell George not to cross Lodge Trail Ridge, where the Indians are likely to lie in ambush. Your husband will be all right."

"I have such a strange foreboding," Frances sobbed as she let Mrs. Carrington lead her to a chair. Sarah and Emmie followed and sat on the sofa beside her. They all soon had a steaming cup of tea and Frances began to calm down.

The door pounded again and Mrs. Wands hurried to answer it. A sergeant stood nervously twisting his cap in his hands. "Colonel Carrington sent me to tell you ladies that a man has come in to tell us that the wood detail has broken corral and reached the Pinery safely. But Fetterman's detail went beyond Lodge Trail Ridge."

Frances cried out at the news of the detail's disobedience of orders, and Mrs. Carrington patted her hand. "George will be all right." Frances relaxed a bit, but she still sat on the edge of her seat. Emmie could tell she was listening to the sounds outside.

The six women chatted and talked about babies and recipes and anything else they could think of. They had a lunch of small sandwiches and stew, but tension still filled the room. They jumped when they heard a shout and a horse go thundering past outside, and they all grabbed their cloaks and went out to the porch. Colonel Carrington dashed down from the lookout and ordered for a howitzer to be readied and gave the order for a general alarm. Men ran in all directions as every man in the garrison reported to the position assigned to him in an extreme emergency.

"What does it mean?" Frances cried out.

"Probably the Indians have been repulsed," Mrs. Carrington said soothingly.

Rooster came scurrying up the steps to the ladies clustered on the porch. "No need to fret, ladies," he said. "Them Sioux bucks won't get ya, I promise."

Then one of the men shouted to open the gate and the colonel's orderly came thundering through on one of the commander's horses. "Reno Valley is full of Indians!" he shouted. "There are several hundred on the road and to the west of it. It was a trap!"

Emmie was standing beside Frances and caught her as she sagged to the ground. "Help me!" she cried to Sarah. The rest of the women clustered around and they got Frances inside and on Mrs. Wands' bed. Mrs. Carrington put a cold cloth to Frances' forehead and she soon came around.

She sat up with a start and burst into tears. "He's dead, I know it," she sobbed.

"Have faith," Mrs. Carrington urged. "Henry sent Captain Ten Eyck out with every man who could be spared. They'll get there in time."

They all went back to the porch. The silence was so intense it was almost painful, then suddenly several shots rang out.

They listened as the shots increased to a frantic pitch, followed by a few rapid volleys, then scattering shots, and finally a dead silence.

"Captain Ten Eyck has repulsed the Indians," Mrs. Carrington said.

Colonel Carrington dashed down from the lookout. Emmie shuddered at the look of dread on his face. She looked at Sarah and saw the same dread reflected on her face. What was happening to their men?

❧

Isaac lay behind an outcropping of rock. They had made it safely to the Pinery, but without reinforcements, they would never make it back to the fort. Rand lay a dozen feet away behind his own rock and Jake several yards beyond his brother behind a tree. Dozens of Indians hid just beyond the rise to the west. They were too well hidden to waste his precious ammunition on. He kept a close eye on the slope as he prayed for reinforcements to be quick. He wasn't quite sure what the Sioux were waiting on. Were they playing a game? It would be dark soon and Indians didn't make war at night.

A volley of shots in the distance rang out. They increased in ferocity for several frantic minutes, then tapered off to an occasional shot before silence descended. Isaac knew that a horrific battle had just taken place, but which side had won? He lifted his head cautiously, then ducked as an arrow sailed by overhead. The arrow was followed by fierce war cries as a band of Sioux rushed toward them.

Rand cried, "Hold your fire until my signal!" Several moments passed. As the band came closer, he gasped, then yelled, "Wolverine!"

The lead Sioux faltered, then pulled his pony to a stop. He shouted something at the rest of the Sioux, and they stopped behind him. He gazed at the rock where Rand lay.

Isaac saw Rand slowly get to his feet. "No, Rand, don't," he whispered.

Rand raised a hand. "Greetings, old friend. I did not think to see you again."

The Sioux dismounted and approached Rand.

"Hold your fire," Rand said again to his fellow soldiers. He stepped forward with his hand outstretched as the young warrior came closer.

Isaac noticed a livid scar running down the cheek of the Sioux as he stopped in front of Rand. *This must be the young brave who rescued Sarah when she was lost in the wilderness after Ben Croftner abducted her,* he thought. He'd heard Sarah talk about Wolverine and White Beaver, the young woman he was pledged to marry. Rand had spared Wolverine's life during a battle once and the two became blood brothers after that.

"I, too, did not think to see my friend again," Wolverine said. The two men gazed at one another for a long moment. "I think many times of my friend with the blue coat and my vow. I watch always in battle to make sure I honor my vow never to fight with my friend."

Rand nodded. "I also watch for my warrior friend. It is good to see you."

The brave grunted. "You in much danger. We will drive the blue coats from the fort by the river. Already many dead beyond the hills." He gestured toward Lodge Trail Ridge.

Isaac looked over at Jake and saw the same alarm on his face. Many killed? Was the relief party dead? What about the fort? Was Emmie safe?

Rand put a hand on Wolverine's shoulder. "What of the fort? Sarah is in the fort."

Wolverine shook his head. "We not attack fort yet. But soon. You go back to fort. Other men come soon to bring you back. Then you must leave fort. I not fight with my brother."

Rand was silent a moment. "I will not fight my brother. But I cannot leave fort unless my commander tells me to."

"Then you must tell him that the Sioux will destroy the fort. We will fight to the last blade and never stop until the blue coats leave our hunting ground."

Rand's hand slid down and gripped Wolverine's hand. "God keep you safe, my brother."

Wolverine gazed into Rand's eyes. "And you, my brother." He turned and walked back to his pony. He vaulted onto his pony, then raised a hand before turning and galloping away. The rest of the band followed.

Isaac got to his feet and he and Jake reached Rand's side at the same time. "The Lord works in strange ways sometimes," Rand said with a distant look on his face. "I knew Wolverine was with Red Cloud, and I always have watched for him. I didn't want to ever break my vow of peace with him."

"Do you think he told you the truth about the rescue party? Could they really be dead?" Jake asked.

The rest of the men were slowly beginning to gather around them. "Don't say anything," Rand said quietly.

A lieutenant slapped Rand on the back. "You must have done some fancy palavering with those savages," he said. "Congratulations."

"I knew him," Rand said shortly. "God worked it all out."

"I don't know about God. Looks like they hightailed it because of reinforcements." He nodded toward the hill, and they turned as Captain Ten Eyck and his men thundered up to them.

Ten Eyck dismounted and ran toward them. "We drove off a band just over the hill. Is everyone all right?"

"Just fine, thanks to you," the lieutenant said. He turned and ordered the men to round up the horses.

"Just be glad you're getting back in one piece," Captain Ten Eyck said quietly. "Fetterman's command wasn't so lucky."

"The relief party?" Rand asked.

Ten Eyck nodded. "Eighty-one men slaughtered and not one left alive. We drove off some Indians and recovered a few bodies, but there are nearly half still out there. The attack on the wood train was a decoy to draw another force out. Thousands of Sioux were hiding just over Lodge Trail Ridge."

The news was so horrific no one responded for several long moments. Eighty-one men! It was almost beyond comprehension. There had never been a slaughter like that in the Indian wars. And thousands of Sioux! Isaac couldn't imagine such a large force of Indians. Two or three hundred was usually considered a large band.

"May God have mercy on their souls," Isaac said finally. "What of the fort?"

"Safe, but we don't know for how long," Captain Ten Eyck said. "Colonel Carrington has readied every mountain howitzer and every available man. But we've been operating with a minimal force and you know how low our ammunition is. So we'd better mount up and get back as quick as we can."

They all hurried off to mount up and get back to the fort. Isaac just wanted to see Emmie with his own eyes and make sure she was safe, and he knew Rand felt the same about Sarah. He glanced at Jake riding beside him. Did he worry about Emmie at all?

≈

The ladies sat around the fire in Mrs. Wands' quarters as night drew on. The evening gun sounded, but the men still weren't back. The colonel's orderly, Sample, had come in some time ago with the news that Reno Valley was full of Indians and nothing could be seen of Fetterman. The entire fort knew some terrible disaster had taken place, but no one knew just what it was.

Emmie wondered what the ladies would do if she suddenly jumped to her feet and shrieked as loud as she could. It was all she could do to hold her terror in check. What if Isaac had been killed? She vaguely wondered how Morning Song was getting along with the baby, but her fear for Isaac's safety wouldn't allow her to leave the little knot of ladies clustered together in a camaraderie of fearful waiting.

The wind whistled outside as the temperature dropped. Rooster had been predicting a blizzard all day, and the weather seemed to be trying to prove him right. Only a few flakes had fallen so far, but the wind was already whipping the existing snow into drifts.

Emmie started to her feet at the sound of a shout outside. She threw her cloak around her and rushed to the door, followed by the rest of the ladies. They all ran toward the gate as doors opened and wagons creaked inside. She saw dead bodies heaped on the wagons and nearly fainted as she searched the mounted men for a glimpse of Isaac's dear face. She breathed a prayer of thanksgiving when she saw Rand, Jake, and Isaac clustered near the last wagon.

The ladies were standing near the flagpole, and Captain Ten Eyck stopped just a few feet away from them where Colonel Carrington stood. His salute was a short, tired wave. "Sir, I'm sorry to report that Fetterman's entire command has been massacred. I brought in all I could, about forty-nine, but there are still more to be claimed."

Frances gasped and started to slide to the ground in a near faint as the ladies overheard Captain Ten Eyck's words. Emmie caught her by the elbow, and she rallied before bursting into tears.

"I knew it," she sobbed. "I just knew he was dead."

Mrs. Carrington put her arms around Frances. "You're coming home with me, dear," she murmured gently as she led her away.

Sarah tugged Emmie's arm. "Let's go home," she said.

Emmie gasped when she saw the dark circles under Sarah's eyes. Her pallor was so pronounced Emmie thought she looked as though she might pass out at any moment. "You're going right home to bed," she said firmly. She took Sarah's arm and steadied her against the wind as they made their way toward their home.

The fire was out when they finally pushed the door shut against the wind. Emmie hurried to start one while Sarah poked the fire in the kitchen stove to life. "I'm going to put on some water for tea," Sarah said. "I can't go to bed until Rand gets home. I couldn't rest anyway until I know what happened."

Joel came in moments later, his young face sober. He silently heaped wood in the fireplace for Emmie, then sat on the floor with his knees drawn up to his chin. The news had quenched even his high spirits.

By the time the men arrived, warm currents from the fire warmed the room and the aroma of steeping tea filled the kitchen. Emmie cut some thick slabs of bread and spread butter and jam on them. She was suddenly ravenous and knew the men would be, too. Morning Song was still at Jake's. Emmie knew the weather was much too cold to have the baby out, but she wished for Morning Song's calming presence. Did she know what had happened?

The door opened and Rand and Isaac dashed in before slamming it against the howling wind. Sarah uttered a little cry and flew into Rand's arms. Emmie was right behind her as she ran to Isaac. She buried her face in the rough wool of his coat and burst into tears.

He put his lips against her hair and patted her on the back. "It's okay," he murmured. "The Lord was looking out for us."

Emmie pulled away and looked up at him. "I'm sorry," she said as she pulled away. What was she thinking of? Unless the Lord intervened, she would be marrying Jake. She had no right to be in Isaac's arms.

Isaac held on a moment, then let her go. "It's not over yet," he said softly as he saw the defeat in her face. "God's in control, you know."

Emmie nodded. "Want some tea and bread?"

"I thought you'd never ask," Isaac said. "I could eat the whole loaf and not know it."

"Me, too," Rand said as he walked toward the kitchen with his arm around his wife.

"Where's Jake?" Sarah asked. "I thought he would come

to see that Emmie was all right. After all, he says he wants to marry her."

"He wanted to see about Gabrielle," Rand said.

Emmie glanced quickly at Isaac. He had come to find her as soon as he could. This was just a taste of what it would be like to be married to a man who didn't love her. Not that she wanted Jake to love her. She couldn't imagine dealing with that problem, too.

Sarah sniffed. "Is he coming over later?"

"No," Rand said. "He said he'd see us in the morning. We're all beat."

Sarah's fierce look softened. "Tell us about it," she invited.

They spent the next hour exclaiming over the harrowing adventure as Rand and Isaac related the day's events.

"I wish you would have asked Wolverine about White Beaver," Sarah said. "I would love to see her again."

"And what about Red Hawk?" Joel put in eagerly. "Did you see him?"

Rand shook his head. "I didn't see Red Hawk and it would have done no good to ask about White Beaver. Even if she were close, you couldn't see her, sweetheart. It's too dangerous to set foot outside the fort. You know that. You haven't been outside the gate since we got here."

Sarah nodded in resignation. "I still wish you'd asked."

Rand grinned. "Well, if we ever get in that situation, I'll be sure to say that my wife has insisted on knowing where his woman is. He'll be very impressed."

Sarah chuckled, then stood. "I'm going to bed. I'll fall asleep right here in this chair if I don't go now. You'd better get to bed too, Joel," she told her brother. Joel didn't complain but went off to his cot in the parlor.

Rand yawned. "Me, too. See you all tomorrow." He stood and followed his wife into the bedroom and shut the door.

"I should be going, too," Isaac said. "It's been a long day."

Emmie stood and followed him to the door.

"Try not to worry," he said. He bent and kissed her on the

forehead. "Things will be all right."

Emmie didn't think so as she shut the door behind him. She just didn't see any way out.

thirteen

The next morning Emmie hurried across the parade ground toward the Carrington residence. It was hard to keep her balance in the driving wind. Already four inches of snow had fallen and if she didn't check on Frances soon, she knew she wouldn't be able to get through the drifts. A pall of dread and foreboding hung over the little fort. She saw sober faces everywhere she looked. The biggest danger, Rand said, was that the Sioux would attack the fort itself. Only the Indians' fear of the big howitzers kept them at bay. If they did attack, all would be lost, because the soldiers were outnumbered and low on ammunition.

Frances was huddled in a quilt on the sofa by the fire when Mrs. Carrington ushered Emmie into the parlor. Frances was pale, but she seemed composed with a strange peace.

"I somehow knew it would come to this," she told Emmie. "George seemed determined to force a fight with the Indians. He idolized Fetterman, but I knew his rashness would come to a bad end. George just wouldn't see it."

Someone knocked at the door again, and Sample, the Carrington's orderly, led in a bearded man in his thirties. He was dressed in civilian clothes so he obviously wasn't a soldier. Emmie thought he might be a scout. He had a wolf robe over his shoulder. He took off his hat and stood turning it in his hands in front of Frances.

"Miz Grummond," he began. "My name is John Phillips. I been a miner and a scout, but I ain't never seen such a bad thing. You been through enough. I'm goin' to Laramie for help for your sake if it costs me my life." He pulled the robe from his shoulder and laid it across Frances' lap. "Here is my wolf robe. I want you to have it to remember me by if I don't make it back."

Frances was nearly speechless, but then she thanked him with tears in her eyes as she stroked the robe.

"Are you going alone?" Emmie asked him.

He shook his head. "Lieutenant Liddle has asked to go, too. We're setting out at different times, though. If one of us don't make it, maybe the other one will get through."

Isaac was going out through a blinding blizzard surrounded by hostile Indians? Why didn't he tell her that last night? "I must go," Emmie said as she fought to keep her composure.

Everyone was assembled in the parlor when she arrived. Jake glanced at her when she came in, then quickly looked away. Isaac, his face set in a stubborn mask, stood stiffly with his back against the fireplace mantle. Sarah looked as though she had been crying.

"So it's true!" Emmie burst out. "You're going to Fort Laramie."

"Someone has to go," Isaac said. "We can't just send Phillips and hope he makes it. Too much is at stake. We have to have reinforcements and ammo. If the Sioux attack, we'll lose the fort itself and everyone in it."

"He's right," Rand said. "Wolverine said the Sioux were planning to attack soon. We can't afford to wait and just hope headquarters will send the reinforcements Colonel Carrington has requested for months now."

"But why does it have to be you?" Emmie asked near tears.

"Why not me?" Isaac said. "I don't have a wife and children here like some of the other men. And I know this terrain. Besides I have the Lord on my side." He said this last with a grin in Emmie's direction.

A bugle sounded at the other end of the fort. "That's assembly," Isaac said. "We have to go." The men all put on their coats and filed out the door. Emmie wanted to run and fling her arms around Isaac one last time, but how could she with Jake there? What if she never saw Isaac again? She struggled against the tears as the door shut against the howling wind.

She must not give in to despair! God was in control. She must trust Him no matter what happened. She whispered a prayer for Isaac's safety as she watched his retreating back through the window.

&

The blizzard had intensified as Isaac, followed by Rand and Jake, fought the wind all the way across the parade ground. The little colonel stood stiffly in front of the assembling men. "I don't have to tell you the urgency of the hour," he said after all the men had fallen into formation. "I need some volunteers to go retrieve our dead comrades. I will not allow the Indians to think we care so little for our fallen that we would leave them for the wolves. They always retrieve their dead no matter what the cost."

Men everywhere lifted their hands eagerly, and he picked out Rand and Jake and ordered them to choose eighty more men to accompany the detail. "I will lead it myself," he said. "It is my duty."

By the time Isaac had assembled his supplies for the trip, the detail to retrieve the dead was nearly ready to leave. John Phillips had already gone ahead, and Isaac wanted to get on his way. He was about to mount up when Jake approached him with a determined look on his face.

"I need to speak with you before you go," Jake said.

Isaac turned and faced his friend. He had tried to hate him for what Jake was doing to him and Emmie, but he couldn't. All Isaac could feel was compassion and pity.

"I know I've been acting like a fool," Jake said. "My brother has been none too gentle about pointing it out to me. I want you to know before you go that I'm releasing Emmie from her promise—if you make it back." He grinned and thrust out his hand. "That's a good incentive for you to fight to get through."

Isaac let out the breath he had been holding. It was just as he'd told Emmie: Be still and let God work it out. "Thank God." He took Jake's hand and pumped it. "It's been hard for me to shut up and let God handle it."

A shadow darkened Jake's face. "Yeah, I've been fighting God. Amelia would be ashamed of me. I've struggled with this thing every night. God wouldn't let me sleep or eat. He just kept telling me like He told Job, 'Where were you when I hung the stars in place?' I don't understand why He would take the one person who gave my life meaning without even letting me say good-bye." Tears glistened in his eyes and he swallowed hard. "But I can't fight Him. He knows best and I just have to trust Him, as hard as it is."

"What will you do with Gabrielle?" Isaac asked. "She still needs a mother." He hesitated, then plunged ahead. "We would be willing to raise her."

"No, but thanks," Jake said firmly. "I'm going to marry Morning Song."

Isaac's eyes widened. "Have you asked her?" he asked slowly.

"No, but I think she'll agree. She loves Gabrielle." He smiled. "You should see Morning Song with her. And her John needs a father." He clapped Isaac on the back. "I don't want to say anything until you get back. If you don't make it, Emmie's baby will need a father and I will honor my promise to Amelia." He said this last with a defiant determination.

"Agreed," Isaac said. "I would want her taken care of." He gripped Jake's hand again. "Whatever happens, will you promise me that you will try to learn to love your new wife? Amelia wouldn't want you to marry just for convenience. She intended for you to be happy."

Jake was silent a moment, then returned the pressure of Isaac's fingers. "All I can say is I'll try. I don't see how I can ever love anyone but Amelia, but I will try."

"That's all I ask," Isaac said. The two men looked at one another a moment. "Take care, Jake. You're not going on any picnic yourself. We don't want a repeat of yesterday."

Jake nodded. "I'll be careful. And Godspeed, my friend. I'll be praying for you."

With a last handshake, Isaac swung up onto Buck and urged him toward the gate. A soldier opened the gate and saluted as he slipped outside into the blinding snow. He had thought long and hard about what would be the best way to accomplish his mission. He decided to avoid obvious trails and travel by night as much as possible. That would help keep him warm during the frigid nights, and with the Lord's help, he could avoid confrontation with the Indians. He had left by a back gate and counted on the Sioux being occupied with celebrating their victory. The detail of men riding out to retrieve the dead would divert the Indians also.

The blizzard intensified out on the plain with no fort walls to block the wind. Isaac's mustache was soon coated with snow and ice, and he wished he had a full beard like many of the men wore. He had to stop often and walk his horse through the snowdrifts. Several hours from the fort, he came to a rock outcropping that offered some protection from the wind, and he decided to try to sleep there until nightfall. He and his horse were both exhausted. Leaving a robe on Buck, he pulled a buffalo robe over himself and fell into a deep sleep punctuated by nightmares of Emmie being dragged away by Sioux hordes. Her eyes were wide with terror, and she screamed his name over and over. When he awoke it was nearly dark. He ate a meal of hardtack and water, then mounted up and started out again.

The blizzard howled around him and the temperature plummeted. Isaac knew it had to be at least twenty or thirty below zero even without the wind. He couldn't feel his fingers or toes, and by morning he could only slump numbly in the saddle. He was so cold and weary he couldn't think, but he forced himself to keep going. The morning only brought a lightening of the gloom as the snow continued to whirl around him. He wasn't even sure he was going in the right direction. He had tried to follow his compass, but the numbing cold made it hard to concentrate. He saw a forlorn cluster of trees to his right and turned Buck's head toward it. A huge snowdrift had formed around them and he thankfully slid to his feet and stumbled toward it. Out of the wind it felt almost warm. He pulled his buffalo robe about him and fell into a dreamless sleep.

When he awoke, the moon was high in the sky and he could see the stars. The snow had quit falling, but the wind still howled. He felt warm, though, and he knew he had to get up and get moving, for he was in danger of freezing. He made himself eat a couple of the crackers he'd brought with him and fed Buck some meager provender. He knocked the ice from his horse's eyes and tail and mounted up.

He found it hard to stay awake as he clung to his saddle pommel. The wind cut through even his buffalo robe, and he swayed in the saddle. *Hang on,* he told himself. *You have to get help for Emmie.* He clutched the saddle pommel with both hands and fought to stay mounted. As his horse rounded a grove of trees, he lost his tenuous grip and pitched sideways from the saddle into a drift. He felt nice and warm away from the wind. *I'll just lay here for a few minutes and rest,* he thought. He closed his eyes and slid into unconsciousness.

❧

December twenty-fourth, Emmie thought as she awoke near dawn. Isaac had been gone three days. She felt an overwhelming need to pray for him. She slipped out of bed and knelt on the cold, hard floor. She shivered as the wind whistled under the door and through her flannel nightgown. If she was cold, what must Isaac be facing? *God, take care of him,* she prayed over and over again. *Only You know where he is and what he needs.*

She was stiff and cold clear through when she finally got up from her knees. She slipped back beneath the covers for a few minutes until she heard the sentry cry, "Five o'clock and all's well."

All's well. No one really believed that. The mood at the fort had been a peculiar one the last few days. Everyone seemed on edge as though they were listening for some sound beyond the log walls of the stockade. Rand and Jake and their detachment had come back two days ago with the rest of the bodies of the slain soldiers. The Indians hadn't bothered them at all. Rand said he wasn't sure if they were holed up in camp because of the blizzard or simply too busy celebrating their victory.

Jake told them that before they left to recover the bodies, Colonel Carrington had opened the magazine and cut the Boorman fuses of round case shot. He opened the boxes of ammunition and adjusted them so that by lighting a single match, the whole lot would go up. His instructions were that if the Indians attacked in overwhelming numbers, the women and children were to be put in the magazine and blown up rather than have any captured alive. Thankfully, that had not happened, but Emmie couldn't forget that the magazine was still readied for such an eventuality.

It had taken several days to dig the grave site in the frozen ground for the slain men. It was so cold the men could only work in fifteen-minute shifts. Joel voiced all their fears when he innocently remarked, "How come they can only work for fifteen minutes when Isaac and John are out in the wind all the time?"

Emmie wondered the same thing. The snowstorm would subside for a few hours, then the snow would swirl down again in a blinding curtain. The soldiers had done all they could to keep a ten-foot trench dug around the stockade. If they had allowed the drifts to pile up, the Indians could have walked right over the tops of the logs in the stockade.

Now here it is Christmas Eve, she thought as she listened to the "All's well." Normally they would be wrapping presents and preparing food for a feast on Christmas Day. She sighed and slipped out of bed again. She pulled on her warmest dress, a worn blue wool one, and quickly combed her hair and washed her face in the cracked bowl on the stand by her bed.

She could try to make Christmas a little festive for Joel and

Sarah, she decided. She would go to Jake's and check on Gabrielle, then see about what she could use for a tree. There were none on the fort grounds, but maybe Joel could find her a branch or something. Joel had been staying at Jake's for appearances' sake, so Morning Song could take care of the baby.

By the time Sarah and Rand came into the kitchen, Emmie had the fire going and the room was beginning to lose its chill. She looked up as Sarah sat down next to her and pulled the teapot over to pour a cup of tea. Rand sat down next to her to pull on his boots.

"Are you all right?" she asked her friend. "You look as though you haven't slept all night."

Sarah sighed. "I'm feeling a bit poorly," she admitted. "My back hurts strangely. The pain seems to come and go."

Emmie narrowed her eyes and looked Sarah over. "I think perhaps Dr. Horton ought to take a look at you," she said. "It could be the baby."

Rand reared his head abruptly. "The baby? It isn't time yet."

"Not quite," Emmie said. "But it's not unusual for one to make his appearance a few weeks early."

"I'll get the doc." Rand didn't argue any more but grabbed his greatcoat and hurried out the door.

"I did wonder," Sarah admitted. "But I didn't want it to be the baby yet. I'm afraid, Emmie." She had tears in her eyes as she looked up. "I don't want to leave Rand and my baby. What if something goes wrong?"

"Don't talk like that," Emmie scolded. "Nothing is going to go wrong. Now you go get undressed and get into bed so the doctor can check you."

Sarah nodded and went to the bedroom. A few minutes later Rand and Dr. Horton opened the door and hurried inside. Both were red-faced from the biting wind. Rand's mustache and the doctor's beard were coated with snow.

Dr. Horton tapped on the bedroom door and went right in. Rand stared blankly at the shut door, then sank down onto a chair. "I'm so afraid, Emmie," he said. "What if—" He broke off his words in midsentence.

Emmie took his hand. "I'll pray with you," she suggested.

Rand smiled wanly. "You are the newest Christian among us, but you sometimes seem like the strongest. I should have thought of that myself."

"I don't have anyone but the Lord," Emmie said softly. "So He's the only one I can turn to."

Rand nodded. "He's our only rock. And He is in control."

They both knelt beside their chairs. "Lord," Rand prayed. "I know we are so undeserving of Your love and care. We sometimes forget how You are always watching out for us and nothing comes to us that doesn't pass through Your hands first. Give us strength to go through what lies before us. Give Sarah strength and courage. If the baby is to come now, guide the doctor's hands and grant us a safe delivery both for Sarah and our baby. Be with me and Emmie that we may be a help and not a hindrance. Amen."

"Amen," Emmie echoed. They got to their feet just as the doctor opened the door and came back into the kitchen.

"The baby's coming," Dr. Horton said. "Unfortunately Sarah is having back labor, so it could be a while. It may help to rub her back, or she may not want you to touch her. It varies with different women. I'll check back in a couple of hours. If the situation changes, send for me."

He left a small bottle of laudanum with them in case the pain got worse. When the door closed behind him, Emmie and Rand went to the bedroom.

Sarah smiled wanly at them. "You were right," she told Emmie.

Emmie smiled and patted Sarah's hand. "Everything will be fine," she told her. "The doctor says it will be a while yet, so why don't you try to rest while you can. We all may have a wonderful Christmas present after all."

"Oh, I hope it doesn't take that long," Sarah moaned as she burrowed deeper under the covers.

Rand and Emmie tiptoed out of the room and shut the door behind them. "I think I'll run over and tell Jake and Joel," Rand said. "Morning Song will want to be here, too. And we may need her."

Emmie nodded. "It wouldn't hurt for Jake to keep you company."

Rand grimaced. "He may not be able to stand it after losing Amelia." He went toward the door. "If Sarah wakes up and asks for me, tell her I'll be right back."

"Try not to worry," Emmie called to his retreating back. She sighed and sat at the table. She was going to need every ounce of strength the Lord could give her. A thousand "what ifs" rang in her head. What if she lost both Isaac and Sarah? She shuddered at the thought. Even losing one would devastate her. She just couldn't think about it. She stood up determinedly. She would keep busy and the day would soon be over. The baby would be here and soon there would be news of Isaac.

By the time she had cleaned the kitchen, Rand was back. Jake, Morning Song, and Joel were with him. Jake had baby Gabrielle wrapped up in a buffalo robe, and her blue eyes peered up at her surroundings as soon as Jake unwrapped her. Joel had carried John over and set him down to play by a bucket of toys on the rug near the fire.

Morning Song took off her cloak and hurried to the bedroom to check on Sarah. "She still sleeping," she announced when she came back out. "That is good. She will need strength."

Emmie walked over to Jake and held out her arms for the baby. Jake kissed his daughter's fuzzy head, then handed her to Emmie and went to sit beside his brother. Everyone seemed quiet and subdued, and Amelia's spirit seemed to hover very near. Emmie knew no one could forget the terrible outcome of Gabrielle's birth. As she cuddled the baby, her own baby moved for the first time in her womb. She gulped and pressed a hand to her stomach. *No one noticed,* she thought with relief as she glanced around the room. Tears pricked her eyes as she thought about what the future held for her and her baby. Everything was such a mess. How could even God work out such a tangled web? She sighed and stood with the baby held close. As she laid her in the cradle near the kitchen stove, she asked God again for strength to face whatever the future held for her and her baby. And for Isaac. Always a prayer for Isaac lay on her heart.

Through the long day Sarah's pains gradually intensified. Joel kept little John occupied while Morning Song and Emmie took turns caring for Gabrielle and tending to Sarah. Dr. Horton popped in several times to check on Sarah's progress. "It will be a while," he kept saying.

Rand and Jake grew quieter and more strained as the day wore on. Several times when Emmie came out of the bedroom, she saw them with their heads bent in prayer. The wind, howling around the corners of the house and whistling through the cracks around the doors and windows, put everyone on edge.

After supper Sarah's labor began in real earnest. Dr. Horton tried to give her a small dose of laudanum, but she refused. She didn't want to risk any harm to the baby, she told him. He snorted, but he put his bottle away without protest.

Emmie was amazed at Sarah's strength and determination. She did not let out one cry when the pains came, but only gripped Emmie's hand tighter. Only an occasional soft groan passed her lips. By ten o'clock the doctor had settled in with them for the night. "It could be any time," he said finally.

Morning Song fed Gabrielle one last time and put her down for the night, then pulled up a chair beside her friend's bed. "Baby come soon now," she announced. She and Emmie took turns bathing Sarah's face with a wet cloth and rubbing her back during the contractions.

Just after midnight on Christmas Day, Sarah gave one last mighty push and a tiny baby boy slid into the world. He squalled in protest when Dr. Horton wiped the mucus away from his nose and mouth. Emmie grinned at the strong, lusty protest. She wrapped him in a bit of flannel and laid him in Sarah's arms.

"Isn't he beautiful?" Sarah asked. She stroked a tender finger down his cheek. "He looks just like his daddy."

"I'll get Rand now," Emmie said. She closed the door behind her and found Rand just outside the door. Joel and John were asleep on a rug by the fire. Jake was sitting at the table with his head in his hands. He and Rand looked pale and haggard. "You have a beautiful son," Emmie said with a smile. "Do you want to see him?"

"How's Sarah?" Rand asked urgently.

"Tired, but just as beautiful as ever," Emmie said.

"Thank God," Jake murmured.

Rand shot through the door, and Sarah cried out and held out her arms to him. He went down on his knees by the bed and buried his face in her hair. She patted him and winked at Emmie as she closed the door behind Morning Song and the doctor.

Jake's knuckles were white as he gripped the table. "I have to go now," he muttered almost incoherently. He grabbed his greatcoat and ran out into the howling wind.

"Wait, Jake," Emmie called, but he just kept on going. She blinked back tears—there was such pain and grief in his eyes.

Morning Song looked at the door for a moment, then bundled the baby up. "I go home with baby," she announced. She wrapped her cloak around her. "Send John home with Joel in morning," she said.

Emmie was too tired to protest at the way it would look if Morning Song spent the night at Jake's alone. He probably wouldn't be there anyway, she told herself as Morning Song slipped out the door.

Rand opened the door and stepped into the kitchen with his small son in his arms. Emmie hurried to him and held out her arms for the tiny scrap. "I think he needs to be cleaned up a bit," she smiled. She had readied some warm water and strips of soft flannel. She had Rand pull the kitchen table close to the stove to keep the baby warm and quickly cleaned the little one and popped him into a gown. He was awake but made no protest at her ministrations. She wrapped him in a flannel blanket and handed him back to his father, who took him eagerly.

Rand gazed down into the face of his son with a look of awe and pride. "Sarah says he looks like me," he said. "But I don't see it."

"Then you must be blind," Emmie said with a laugh. "Look at that nose. And he has your dimples."

Just then the baby yawned and moved his mouth in such a way that Rand saw his dimples for the first time. "You're right," he said excitedly. "Ma will be so excited to hear about him."

"Maybe your family can come for a visit soon," Emmie said. "This may be all it takes to heal the breach with your father."

A shadow darkened Rand's brow. "I wouldn't hold my breath," he said shortly. "Pa is determined that I give up what he calls my foolishness and come back to the farm. Ma says he doesn't mention my name."

"A grandchild can change everything," Emmie said.

"Maybe," Rand said with a shrug.

There was a sound from the parlor, then Joel came flying into the kitchen. His red hair stood on end as he slid to a stop in front of Rand and the baby. "Let me see," he begged.

Rand grinned and pulled back the blanket to reveal the baby. "Meet your new nephew."

Joel gave a sigh of awe. "Can I hold him?"

Rand passed him over to the young boy. "He's going to be pestering you unmercifully before you know it," he teased.

"I'm going to be the best uncle there ever was," Joel promised in a hushed tone. "I'm going to teach him all kinds of things, like where the best fishing spot is and how to play baseball." He looked up from his perusal of his nephew with a sudden look of alarm. "How's Sarah? She's all right, isn't she?"

Rand nodded toward the bedroom door. "See for yourself."

Joel carried the baby to the bedroom as Emmie opened the door for him. Sarah looked asleep, but she opened her eyes as soon as Joel stepped into the room. She smiled when she saw her brother with her baby. "Did Rand tell you what we named him?" she asked.

Joel shook his head. "I forgot to ask," he said with a sheepish look.

Sarah laughed. "His name is Joshua Joel Campbell," she said.

Joel gaped, then his chest swelled with importance. "Man alive," was all he could say. "If that don't beat the dutch."

Rand clapped a hand on his shoulder. "If he turns out as good a boy as his namesake, we'll be very pleased."

Tears welled up in Joel's eyes at such praise from the man he adored. "I'll try to be a good example," he promised.

Sarah yawned, and Emmie saw the weariness behind her friend's smile. "It's time for the new mama to get some rest," she said. She shooed everyone out of the bedroom and put little Joshua in his cradle.

Sarah smiled sleepily at her as she plumped the pillows and straightened the covers. "I did good, didn't I?" she asked.

"You did good," Emmie assured her. "We're all very proud of you."

Sarah smiled again and was asleep before Emmie could close the door behind her. Rand and Joel were asleep in the parlor, Rand on the cot and Joel on the rug by the fire. As Emmie crawled into her cold bed, she thanked God that He had brought them safely through and asked again that He watch over Isaac.

fourteen

The next few days were the oddest Emmie could ever remember. On one hand they were all so excited and relieved that Sarah and the baby were all right, and on the other they held their breath as they waited for the Sioux to make their next move. No one had to tell the women that if the Sioux chose to attack, the fort would fall. Ammunition was dangerously low and no one ventured outside the stockade except for the detail of men to keep the trench around the wall clear.

One night around midnight a general alarm sounded and Rand rushed out into the night. They had huddled around the fire and prayed for nearly an hour as they listened to the shouts and the boom of the howitzer as the soldiers rallied to the rescue of a corralled wagon train. When Rand returned, he grimly told them the train had brought an official notice of perfected peace, with instructions to freely make presents to the Indians. No wonder headquarters had not sent ammunition and extra troops when the colonel had requested it weeks earlier. Everyone evidently believed that falsehood.

The weather continued to hover between minus twenty-five and minus forty. Emmie and Sarah both longed for the company of the other women in the fort, but beyond a brief visit from Frances and Mrs. Horton the day after Joshua made his appearance, no one ventured beyond their own four walls. Finally New Year's Day ushered in a slight break in the weather and the entire fort gathered for a brief memorial service for the slain men. As Emmie looked around at the faces gathered around the parade ground, the gravity of their situation was evident on every countenance. No one knew if they would all end up as the poor massacred men, but with no one left to bury their remains and speak a last prayer over them.

Mrs. Horton had to support poor Frances, who was nearly fainting from the stress and grief.

Two days into the new year, Emmie sat at the kitchen table up to her elbows in flour as she kneaded bread. Sarah, nursing the baby at the kitchen table, looked up as a bugle call sounded. Emmie, her fingers deep in bread dough, froze as the bugle sounded the long roll that meant troops had been spotted. Her hand to her breast, she held her breath as she rose and listened more closely. The bugle sounded again and she bolted toward the door.

"Stay there," she told Sarah as she threw her cloak around her and ran out the door. From every home, people poured out the doors with looks of dawning hope. Jake ran past her and she grabbed at his arm.

"Fresh troops are almost here," he told her. "Phillips or Isaac made it through!"

Tears of relief flooded her eyes as she ran to stand beside Frances. Even Jessica and her mother were out, she noticed. Jessica saw her stare and turned her back. The troops flooded through the gates. Emmie thought they all looked nearly frozen. Most had frostbite patches of white on their cheeks, their mustaches and beards were thickly caked with snow and ice, and they all wore a look of intense suffering. Desperate to find Isaac, she looked frantically through the milling men and horses, but there was no familiar grin or shock of red hair.

Colonel Carrington stood off to one side, talking to the major who had led the men. After several minutes, he came to where the women were. "Phillips made it through on Christmas Day," he told them. "It has taken this long for them to get through the blizzard."

"What about Isaac?" Emmie asked anxiously.

Colonel Carrington shook his head. "I'm sorry, my dear. He never showed up at the fort."

Emmie caught her breath. She clenched her hands beneath the folds of her cloak. He must be mistaken! Of course Isaac made it through. He was wrong. She searched the colonel's face, but she saw only compassion and understanding. He thought Isaac was dead, she realized. She took a step back.

"No, you're wrong," she stammered. She turned and ran across the parade ground. She'd find Rand, she thought. He'd know the truth. She found him giving directions to the men assigned to unpack the stores of supplies the troops had brought.

"Rand, I can't find any news of Isaac," she told him.

He put an arm around her and drew her off to one side. She looked up into his brown eyes and saw grief. She put her hands on his chest and pushed. "No, you're wrong," she said. "He's not dead. I'd know if he were dead."

Rand pulled her to him and held her. "You're strong now, Emmie, and you've got to face the facts. He didn't make it. He was a brave soldier, and he'd want you to be brave now, too."

She wept against the rough wool of his jacket, but everything felt unreal. Isaac couldn't be dead. She couldn't accept that.

"Let me take you home," Rand said. He led her across the parade ground as she walked woodenly back to their quarters. Sarah saw the look of desolation in her eyes as she came in and stood up with a cry. She held out her arms and Emmie flew into them.

The next few days passed in a haze of grief and bewilderment. *How could it all end this way?* she wondered. She knew now how Jake felt when he lost Amelia. When Jake told her grimly that the plans for their marriage were moving ahead, she just nodded numbly. What did any of it matter now that Isaac was gone?

ફ*ર*

Isaac stirred and licked his lips. He was so very thirsty. He sat up and stared at the fireplace across the room. Where was he? The last thing he clearly remembered was pitching into a snowbank. He had vague impressions of the dark face of an old man that swam in and out of sight and dim memories of tossing and crying out feverishly.

A door opened and the man in Isaac's dreams came through it. He was short and husky with a beard clear to his chest and black matted hair. He wore a faded red flannel shirt, stained and patched in numerous places, and trousers so dirty it was hard to tell what their original color had been. He squinted at Isaac, then spat a stream of tobacco juice on the floor.

"Awake, are ye?" he said with a scowl. "What in creation were ye doing wandering around in a blizzard?"

"What day is it?" Isaac struggled to swing his feet over the edge of the cot.

"Don't believe in answering questions?" the man asked. "That ain't polite."

"I've got to get to Fort Laramie. It's a matter of life and death." Isaac stood and swayed weakly. He leaned against the wall until his head stopped spinning.

"It was pert near your death," the man remarked. "Ye was as close to freezing to death as I'd ever seen. And the fever that followed about finished the job. It's a ways to Laramie. What's so all fired important? I can see ye is a soldier."

Isaac nodded. "There's been a bloody massacre at Fort Phil Kearney. We need ammo and men or we'll lose the fort itself and every man, woman, and child in it." He sat back down on the edge of the cot and leaned over to pull on his boots. "Where's my horse?"

"Not so fast. Ye can't light out again without some vittals. All ye've eaten is a little broth I was able to get down ye. Ye would never make it past the corral." He pointed to the table. "Sit down and fill your belly. The wind is still screaming like a banshee. The soup will warm ye."

Isaac eyed the steaming bowl. He was ravenous, he discovered. He started toward the table and staggered weakly. What was wrong with him? He sat down and bowed his head and thanked God for the food and for saving his life.

When he looked up, the man was staring at him. "Ye are a God-fearing man," he said. "I ain't seen nobody pray since my mam pert near forty years ago." He was silent a moment, then said, "My name's Pete Sweeney but folks call me Hardtack." He cackled and pushed the bowl of stew toward Isaac. "I reckon cause they think I'm as tough as old shoe leather."

Isaac picked up a bent and tarnished spoon and dug into the stew. The smell made his mouth water. "Lieutenant Liddle," he mumbled between bites. "How far are we from Fort Laramie?"

" 'Bout a day's ride on a fresh horse," Hardtack said. "Which yer horse ain't. He was as near dead as you. Just now startin' to perk up some."

"You got a fresh horse?" Isaac wiped the last of the stew with a crust of bread and stood up.

"Naw. I got an old mule named Bertha, but she ain't good for much but carrying a light load downhill," the old man said.

"What day is it?" Isaac asked again.

Hardtack scratched his grizzled head. "I don't rightly know," he said. "The days all run together out here." He stood and walked to a faded dirty calendar nailed to the wall by the door. "Let's see, this is the day I went for supplies and it took me seven days coming back. I found you here and that were six days ago."

"Six days!" Isaac broke in. "I've been here six days?"

The old man continued as though Isaac had not interrupted. "January second," Hardtack said. "Near as I can figure."

"I've got to get to Laramie." Isaac jumped to his feet and looked around him. "Where're my boots?"

"Under the bed." Hardtack pointed a gnarled finger.

Isaac grabbed his boots and feverishly began to pull them on. "I even missed Christmas," he muttered to himself. He'd had such special plans for Emmie. His mother's engagement ring was hidden back in his room, waiting for the right moment to give it to her.

"Christmas, huh?" the old man said. "I ain't thought about Christmas since I were a boy. Ain't no one to give no presents to out prospecting anyhow." He shook his finger at Isaac.

"Now I'm telling ye, ye can't go nowhere just yet. Ye need to get your strength back."

"I can't wait that long," Isaac said frantically. "I have to get reinforcements." He began to search for his greatcoat and buffalo robe.

Hardtack sighed and pointed to the other side of the bed, where he'd piled Isaac's belongings. "If ye are bent on killing yourself and your horse, I reckon I can't stop ye."

Isaac looked at the old man a moment, then at an inner urging, rummaged through his knapsack and found his small New Testament. "Can you read?" he asked the old man.

Hardtack bristled. " 'Course I can read. What ye take me for? Some kind of half-wit? My mam was very particular 'bout all us young 'uns knowing about reading and writing."

"Then I'd like to say thanks for saving my life with this." Isaac gently handed him the small black book. "It's the most precious thing I own."

Hardtack blinked, then slowly reached out a hand and took the book. "My mam had one like this," he said in a quavering voice. He stroked the battered cover. "Why would ye give me such a thing?"

"God told me to," Isaac said.

The old man blinked back tears. "Thank ye kindly," he said. "I'll take good care of it."

When Isaac left, Hardtack had pulled a chair near the fire and sat engrossed in the contents of the small black book.

Isaac staggered weakly through the drifts of snow to the shed surrounded by a rickety corral. How was he going to get through when he was so weak? He grimly pushed on. He had to make it. God would give him the strength somehow.

He found Buck bedded down in a heap of straw with an old blanket thrown over him. "Sorry, boy," he said. "We've got to get on the road again." He slipped the bit into Buck's mouth and hurriedly saddled him. He led him out the door into the wind-driven snow. After swinging up into the saddle, he tucked his buffalo robe securely around him, checked his compass, and dug his heels into Buck's flank.

He felt he was close enough to Fort Laramie to travel in the daylight. This close to the fort most of the Indians were friendly Brulé Sioux. It was still slow going in the drifting snow, but Isaac felt a new strength coursing through him, a new optimism. He was going to make it! He just prayed that God would protect the fort with His mighty right hand until help could arrive.

After riding nearly three hours, he began to recognize the terrain. He was almost to Fort Reno! Maybe they would have news of Fort Phil Kearny. A sentry stopped him as he rode up, then opened the gate. He made his way to the commanding officer's headquarters and knocked on the door.

"Enter," the commander called.

He stepped inside and saluted the major seated behind a scarred, makeshift desk. "Sir, I come with a dispatch from Colonel Carrington at Fort Phil Kearny. There's been a terrible battle and we desperately need reinforcements and ammunition."

The major waved his hand. "Where have you been, Lieutenant? We got word of the massacre days ago. Troops should just about be there by now."

Isaac sagged in relief. The fort was saved! "I had some bad luck, Major. I'm just thankful Phillips made it through."

The major nodded. "You don't look well, Lieutenant. You'd better head to mess and get some chow."

Isaac opened his mouth to object and say he was going back to Fort Phil Kearny, when the major interrupted him.

"That's an order, Lieutenant."

Isaac sighed. It seemed he didn't have a choice. He saluted, then left headquarters and made his way across the tiny parade ground to the mess hall. After a bowl of stew and a stringy piece of meat, he mounted up and pointed Buck's head back to Fort Phil Kearny.

❧

Sarah coaxed Emmie's hair into soft ringlets with the aid of the hot tongs. "You're going to be a beautiful bride," she told her.

Emmie forced a smile. "I doubt if Jake really cares how I look," she told her. "As long as I show up, he'll be content."

Morning Song peeked in the bedroom where the other two women were. "There you are, my friend. I bring you something for luck." She held out a beautifully beaded belt.

"Oh, Morning Song, it's lovely," Emmie said. She took the belt and examined it. The belt had tiny eagle designs with exquisite detailing. She hugged her friend and slipped the belt around her waist. It looked beautiful against the cream of her dress.

Morning Song sat on the edge of the bed. "Jake tell me to go make woman talk," she said with a shy smile. "He walk and pace like a panther."

The women chuckled. "Rand said Jake was nervous," Sarah said. "You wouldn't think so since he's been through it before."

They all fell silent at the oblique reference to Amelia. Emmie felt tears prick her eyes. She still missed Amelia and knew the pain was a never-ending one for Sarah, too. Poor Jake. She knew she could never make up to him all he'd lost, but perhaps they could find some measure of happiness together in raising Gabrielle and the baby Emmie carried.

"I wish you much happiness, my sister," Morning Song said with downcast eyes.

Emmie looked at her lovely face and wished things could have been different. She had felt for some time that Morning Song harbored warm feelings for Jake. And sometimes she saw a softness in Jake when he looked at Morning Song. *Not love yet, but it could have blossomed,* Emmie thought. If there had just been the opportunity.

She finished her toilet, and the three women pulled on their cloaks, bundled up the baby, and hurried across the parade ground to the little chapel. Once inside the foyer, Sarah handed Joshua to Morning Song, then repaired the damage the wind had wrought and put the filmy veil on Emmie's head. Morning Song slipped inside the door and sat at the back of the chapel with baby John.

Sarah looked into the chapel and motioned for the post band to begin the music, then stepped out and took Rand's arm as he escorted her to front of the chapel where they would stand up with Emmie and Jake.

Emmie took a deep breath and walked slowly down the aisle. She didn't look to the left or the right as she fixed her eyes on the preacher, but she was aware of the many eyes on her. Most of the fort, including Maggie, the laundress, and the enlisted men, had turned out for the wedding. Everyone was grateful for a chance to forget the bad time they'd all been through. She didn't look at the broad back of the man who waited for her. She knew she would burst into tears when she saw Jake there where Isaac was supposed to be. She stopped in front of the preacher with her head down. Warm fingers clasped hers, and she jumped a little at the gentle pressure. Perhaps Jake was beginning to feel some small affection for her.

"Dearly beloved," the pastor began. His voice droned on as Emmie blocked most of it out. Then he said, "Emmaline Croftner, do you take this man to be your wedded husband? Will you love him, honor and obey him, and cling to him only as long as you both shall live?"

The words pounded in her head and she turned to meet the gaze of the man who would be her husband. Familiar blue eyes met hers, and she gasped and closed her eyes. She was hallucinating for sure. She opened one eye cautiously to see a familiar grin.

Isaac caught her as she started to slide to the floor. "I thought you'd be glad to see me," he said.

It was Isaac! She looked around to see the smiling faces of her friends. Even Jake was grinning. She couldn't remember the last time she saw him smile.

"Surprise!" Sarah hugged her. "He made it back late this morning, just in time to switch places with Jake. I just found out myself. Aren't you going to answer the preacher?"

Emmie looked in bewilderment at the minister, who smiled complacently back at her.

"Well, are you going to marry me or not?" Isaac asked.

Jake nodded at her. "I've released you from your promise," he said. "And if Morning Song is agreeable, we'll make it a double wedding." He looked back at Morning Song and held out his hand. Her eyes never leaving his, she stood and handed John to Frances Grummond before walking to Jake and putting her small brown hand in his. Jake turned and faced the minister again. "Let's get this wedding moving along. I'm ready for some cake."

With her hand in Isaac's, looking into his warm blue eyes, Emmie knew the Lord her God had done this wondrous thing. Her heart overflowing with love and joy, she repeated her vows, then stepped into Isaac's arms.

epilogue

Emmie looked around the nearly bare rooms where she'd spent the last two years. Was she leaving anything behind? This would be the last time she would ever see these rooms again. Sap no longer oozed from the rough logs, and the tiny rooms looked barren without their gay calico curtains and tablecloths. Dust motes danced in the hot summer sunshine that filled the parlor.

The treaty of 1868 had agreed to abandon Forts Reno, C.F. Smith, and Phil Kearny to the Indians. No one would ever inhabit these walls again. Isaac said the Indians would burn the fort as soon as the soldiers were out of sight.

She looked down at a tug on her skirt. Tiny Amelia, just over two, lifted her arms up to be held. Smiling, Emmie knelt and took the child in her arms. She buried her face in her daughter's sweet-smelling hair. God had blessed her so much. Amelia's birth had been easy, and the joy the little girl brought to both her and Isaac was simply amazing. Who would have thought that she would have so much just three years after she had heard the shriek of the overturning carriage that day in Wabash?

Life was good. Even Jake seemed to have finally put the past behind him. He looked at Morning Song with love in his eyes now. They were expecting an addition to their little family in October. Sarah had given Rand another son last year and was also expecting a new baby around Christmas. She and Rand had said they wanted a large family and they were well on their way to having their dreams fulfilled. Emmie had even had an opportunity to tell her brother Labe about how God had changed her life when he'd stopped by three months ago on his way back to the gold fields of Bozeman.

He had brought news about Ben's death in a shooting during a poker game with other miners. Emmie had been sad, but not surprised. Ben had too much pride to ever bend his knee to God.

Emmie whirled now as the front door banged shut and her husband strode in. Isaac smiled as he caught sight of her with Amelia in her arms.

"It won't be long before you won't be able to pick her up," he said, glancing at the gentle bulge where their new baby grew. Amelia held out her arms to him and he took her and tossed her into the air.

She giggled. "Again, Daddy," she cried.

Emmie watched as Isaac played with Amelia. He was never too busy to take a moment to bring a smile to the little girl's face. He had certainly kept his promise to be a good father. And husband. She loved him with a fierce, almost painful love.

His deep voice interrupted her introspection. "Are you ready to leave?"

Emmie linked her arm through his and gazed up into his blue eyes. "I'm ready," she said. He opened the door and they walked across the parade ground for the last time.

"Bye, bye, house," little Amelia called, waving her chubby hands.

Emmie echoed the sentiment in her heart as Isaac helped her up into their wagon and then handed Amelia to her. A new fort and a new home awaited them in Arizona. She remembered the words of Ruth, "Whither thou goest, I will go; and where thou lodgest, I will lodge; thy people shall be my people, and thy God my God: Where thou diest, will I die, and there will I be buried."

She would follow Isaac wherever the army sent them, and she would go happily. It was more than she'd ever hoped for and it was good.

A Letter To Our Readers

Dear Reader:

In order that we might better contribute to your reading enjoyment, we would appreciate your taking a few minutes to respond to the following questions. We welcome your comments and read each form and letter we receive. When completed, please return to the following:

Rebecca Germany, Fiction Editor
Heartsong Presents
PO Box 719
Uhrichsville, Ohio 44683

1. Did you enjoy reading *Plains of Promise?*
   ❑ Very much. I would like to see more books
   by this author!
   ❑ Moderately
   I would have enjoyed it more if _____

   _____

   _____

2. Are you a member of **Heartsong Presents**? Yes ❑ No ❑
   If no, where did you purchase this book?_____

   _____

3. How would you rate, on a scale from 1 (poor) to 5 (superior), the cover design?_____

4. On a scale from 1 (poor) to 10 (superior), please rate the following elements.

   _____ Heroine   _____ Plot

   _____ Hero   _____ Inspirational theme

   _____ Setting   _____ Secondary characters

5. These characters were special because_____

_____

_____

6. How has this book inspired your life?_____

_____

_____

7. What settings would you like to see covered in future
   Heartsong Presents books?_____

_____

_____

8. What are some inspirational themes you would like to see
   treated in future books?_____

_____

_____

9. Would you be interested in reading other **Heartsong
   Presents** titles?   Yes ❑   No ❑

10. Please check your age range:
    ❑ Under 18   ❑ 18-24   ❑ 25-34
    ❑ 35-45   ❑ 46-55   ❑ Over 55

11. How many hours per week do you read?_____

Name _____

Occupation _____

Address _____

City _____ State _____ Zip _____

Discover the joy of love...

A nostalgic look at springtimes past, and the joy of love discovered. *Spring's Memory* is the latest collection of historical inspirational novellas from Barbour Publishing. Includes the stories *A Valentine for Prudence* by Darlene Mindrup, *Set Sail My Heart* by Colleen Coble, *The Wonder of Spring* by Carol Cox, and *The Blessings Basket* by Judith McCoy Miller.

400 pages, Paperbound, 5 ³/₁₆" x 8"

❤ ❤ ❤ ❤ ❤ ❤ ❤ ❤ ❤ ❤ ❤ ❤ ❤ ❤ ❤ ❤ ❤ ❤

❤ ❤ ❤ ❤ ❤ ❤ ❤ ❤ ❤ ❤ ❤ ❤ ❤ ❤ ❤ ❤ ❤ ❤

·····Hearts♥ng·····

HISTORICAL ROMANCE IS CHEAPER BY THE DOZEN!

Buy any assortment of twelve *Heartsong Presents* titles and save 25% off of the already discounted price of $2.95 each!

Any 12 *Heartsong Presents* titles for only $26.95 *

*plus $1.00 shipping and handling per order and sales tax where applicable.

HEARTSONG PRESENTS TITLES AVAILABLE NOW:

(If ordering from this page, please remember to include it with the order form.)

·········Presents·········

Great Inspirational Romance at a Great Price!

Heartsong Presents books are inspirational romances in contemporary and historical settings, designed to give you an enjoyable, spirit-lifting reading experience. You can choose wonderfully written titles from some of today's best authors like Peggy Darty, Sally Laity, Tracie Peterson, Colleen L. Reece, Lauraine Snelling, and many others.

When ordering quantities less than twelve, above titles are $2.95 each.
Not all titles may be available at time of order.

SEND TO: Heartsong Presents Reader's Service
P.O. Box 719, Uhrichsville, Ohio 44683

Please send me the items checked above. I am enclosing $_____.
(please add $1.00 to cover postage per order. OH add 6.25% tax. NJ add 6%). Send check or money order, no cash or C.O.D.s, please.
To place a credit card order, call 1-800-847-8270.

NAME _____

ADDRESS _____

CITY/STATE_____ ZIP _____

Hearts♥ng Presents

Love Stories Are Rated G!

That's for godly, gratifying, and of course, great! If you love a thrilling love story, but don't appreciate the sordidness of some popular paperback romances, **Heartsong Presents** is for you. In fact, **Heartsong Presents** is the *only inspirational romance book club*, the only one featuring love stories where Christian faith is the primary ingredient in a marriage relationship.

Sign up today to receive your first set of four, never before published Christian romances. Send no money now; you will receive a bill with the first shipment. You may cancel at any time without obligation, and if you aren't completely satisfied with any selection, you may return the books for an immediate refund!

Imagine. . .four new romances every four weeks—two historical, two contemporary—with men and women like you who long to meet the one God has chosen as the love of their lives. . .all for the low price of $9.97 postpaid.

To join, simply complete the coupon below and mail to the address provided. **Heartsong Presents** romances are rated G for another reason: They'll arrive *Godspeed!*